Over The Falls In A Suitcase

By Kathleen Vincenz

To my family, who endured the Falls in a brisk, cold November and even caught my suitcase.

CONTENTS

1 PUPPIES! BUT …   7

2 WAITING   11

3   NO MORE WAITING   18

4 PACKING UP PINK   28

5 LEAVING IN STYLE   34

6 WHAT'S FOR BREAKFAST?   39

7 WE'RE HERE   46

8 ADVENTURES IN GRANDEUR   50

9 MOVING ON UP   56

10 WHAT A MESS!   63

11 ROARING THROUGH THE LION   72

12 CATCHING THE LION   81

13 LOSING HEART   90

14 BALLROOMS, BOYS, AND SINGING   100

15 IT'S ONLY MAKE BELIEVE   109

16 FINDING MORE THAN EXPECTED   117

17 SEARCHING FOR ANSWERS   125

18 THE MIRACLE OF LIFE   132

19   DECIDING   143

EPILOGUE – TEN WEEKS OF WAITING ENDS   147

PUPPIES! BUT ...

Lindsey reached her finger into the cage and tickled the nose of the nearest puppy, a fluff of silky black fur with a red tongue. The other puppies barked and squirmed, bumping into each other in their excitement to reach her. She tingled to grab one and run home. The sign on the cage read *Cockapoos--$1,250 each*. Imagine paying that much for a dog. She and Jenna didn't even want a Cockapoo, but she could change her mind.

"Lindsey!"

Lindsey braced herself as Jenna careened into her, shaking the cage of puppies on the red and yellow linoleum floor of the PetFarm. The puppies yipped and barked in response.

"You left Lacy's!" Jenna bounced on her pink shoes, her blue jacket falling off her skinny shoulders. "Didn't you hear Mom calling you? You're toast."

"I only went here to PetFarm. One store away." Lindsey twisted her brown hair and pulled it behind her ear. "And, no, I didn't hear Mom."

But she had heard her—she'd called to Lindsey but Lindsey had to get away. Her face heated to 100 degrees at the thought of her cosmetics shopping. Oh, why could she never decide?

"Look at you!" Jenna pointed at Lindsey's eyes, then covered her mouth and giggled. "You're a clown. How many colors do you have on?"

"Is it that bad? The lady kept dragging out more and more eye shadows and putting them on me." Lindsey thought of how long she'd stared at the back of the woman as the woman dug for yet another color. Then, the woman would turn around with her deep black charcoal-lined eyes, and her lips dripping in scarlet. Her name tag read, *Gertrude, Cosmetic Specialist.* "She wouldn't listen."

"You probably let her boss you. Look for yourself. Here's my mirror." Jenna dug for her poodle-shaped mirror.

Lindsey studied her face in it. Shocking purple eyelids blazed above her otherwise unadorned face, making her look even plainer and younger than fourteen with her brown hair drooping down her back.

"You didn't buy that stupid color, did you?" Jenna laughed into her hand. "Dad'll be so mad."

Lindsey shook her head, fingering the $20 bill in the pocket of her gray coat that Aunt Angie had given her. She thought of how the cosmetics woman had waved her hand over the dozen of opened eye shadows strewn on the counter, and shouted, *"You're not going to buy anything, are you?"* And, Lindsey had run here to PetFarm.

"I bought this." Jenna touched the new purple lace headband she wore with a yellow flower blooming on top. Her ruler-straight hair hung down her skinny back. She sighed. "I had a good shopping experience, lots of positive karma. Oh, but look at these puppies. Aren't they the cutest, sweetest, most adorable things?" Jenna stuck her finger in to the cage and the largest puppy—about the size of a football—licked it. Jenna laughed. "Its little tongue is rough and yet its fur is soft. But we want a Yorkshire Terrier, and these cost a gazillion dollars."

"Yeah, I know. They *are* cute though." Lindsey petted the nearest puppy, her finger entwining in his curls. "Do you think we'd ever get that kind of money?"

"No, but let's pretend we do and choose the one we want. What about that one—" Jenna pointed to the biggest puppy. "Strong, good stock."

"Oh, I don't know, how about the little one? He likes it when you tickle his nose." Lindsey rubbed his nose and laughed.

Just then, Gwen appeared behind them. "What are you doing? Mom and Dad are mad—absolutely furious." Her arms overflowed with store bags emblazoned with *Lacy's, Where the Magic is for Christmas*. She wore a headband like Jenna's. Lindsey could tell she'd arranged her hair so her natural blonde streak that ran through her brown hair showed the best.

"I only followed Lindsey here." Jenna pouted. "Don't blame me."

"And, I only needed to get away from the, well, shopping." Lindsey twisted her hair with her finger into a tight knot.

"Look at your eyes! Great shopping." Gwen dropped her bags with a crash to the floor. "You better wipe that stuff off before Dad sees. I'm the only one allowed eye shadow. You can't cheat and do stuff earlier than me. Sixteen is the deal with Dad. And my green eyes would look good with purple, not your brown."

When Gwen said this, Mom stood in the doorway of PetFarm, pale and trembling, her light-brown eyes searching for them. "Lindsey!" Her voice quivered as she called again, "Lindsey! Girls! What are you ..." She stepped forward barely avoiding the door swinging behind her. She swayed and held her hand to her face. "Oh, dear, I think I'm going to ..." She stumbled backward. Like a super hero, Dad rushed in and caught her. She collapsed against him.

"Mom fainted!" Jenna cried. "You did it, Lindsey."

Dad, his face flaring redder than his hair, moved toward them, assisting Mom. "Clear a place for your mother!"

Gwen swept collars and leashes off of a table and Dad sat Mom on it. She slumped forward on the edge, her head in her hands. Her black curly hair lay flat and sweaty on her forehead like she'd been to exercise class. Dad gripped her hand. Lindsey flashed back to last week when she'd seen Mom crying in the bathroom.

"We've got to get your mother home." Dad gently pulled Mom to stand, but she fell against him. He swept her up in his arms as if they were on their honeymoon.

"It'll be OK, Dad." Jenna rushed toward the door of PetFarm. "I'll push the handicap button. It'll keep the door wide open." Jenna's hand hovered over the silver mushroom-shaped button with a picture of a wheel chair on it. "It's how it's been designed. Besides, I've always wanted to push it."

"Quiet, Jenna." Gwen shoved Jenna out of the way. "Act your age, I'll hold the door."

"Lindsey," Jenna cried. "We should push the handicap button, right?"

Lindsey shrugged keeping her shoulders high. She didn't know. She never knew what to do in an emergency.

"Jenna, don't be silly," Gwen said. "Mom will be *crushed* when the door closes before she gets through, and it'll be your fault." Gwen pulled the door open, and Jenna ran back to Lindsey, bumping her in the back. Lindsey wasn't sure if it was an accident or not.

"Lindsey," Jenna cried. "Why didn't you defend my way?"

Mom lifted her head from Dad's shoulder. "See, Joe, how they're acting?" Dad nodded in agreement. "They can't even work together to open a door. We'll have to follow through on our decision." She hung her head and a sob escaped. He raised her hand to his lips and kissed it.

Lindsey trembled in fear as she followed her family out of the glass doors and into the cold parking lot, all of them in a quiet procession, even Gwen and Jenna. The branches of the trees, their leaves finally gone, etched against the murky November sky. Why wasn't Halloween in November? A November sky certainly was spookier than an October one, especially tonight.

"Where's the car?" Jenna asked.

Dad didn't hesitate. He marched down the row to their white station wagon. Gwen took the car keys from him and unlocked the doors. Lindsey could smell his sharp cologne as he lifted Mom into the car, rust chinking off when he rubbed his arm against the door.

Driving off with her family, she knew she'd never forget the horrid confusion in her head and the dread in her soul. What was happening to Mom? And, h

WAITING

A half an hour later, Lindsey and her sisters sat stiff and uncomfortable around their dark oval kitchen table waiting for Dad to come downstairs. An empty chair separated them so they couldn't touch each other. When they'd gotten home, Dad had growled at them, "Sit!" He'd been so angry that Mom had shaken in his arms when he spoke. "I'll deal with you later."

Lindsey had rushed to her chair feeling her face redden with embarrassment and fear, while Gwen had acted as if she didn't care, taking the time to brush crumbs off her chair before sitting, and Jenna had tumbled into hers. Now they were waiting for whatever anger was left in him.

Lindsey tried not to think about Mom upstairs, and instead traced the deep scratch that ran though the table like a river. Jenna had carved it with her first pair of sharp scissors. Lindsey traced the scratch until her hand reached Gwen's space. Gwen slapped her hand back.

"Ow, Gwen!" Lindsey said. "I'm just trying to keep occupied."

"Twiddle your thumbs."

Lindsey wiggled her thumbs in the air. "I would if I knew what *that* meant."

"Don't do it!" Jenna held her hands in the air. "You'll get thumb muscles—your thumbs will be thick!"

"Oh, Jenna!" Lindsey stared at her thumbs. "That can't be true."

"Stop it. You're both idiots." Gwen put her head in her hands. "No wonder we can't get along. I don't need to use physical things to keep me occupied—I use my intellect. I'm reciting French love poems to myself right now."

Gwen mouthed something French, then examined her nails and tugged at a hangnail. She patted her hair pulling on her natural blonde streak, and picked lint off of her purple sweater.

"Oh, I am too." Jenna scratched the top of her head with her fingers, and wiggled around. She licked her lips and sang, "*Frère Jacques, Frère Jacques!*"

"Girls!" Dad called down the stairs. "What is going on down there?"

Lindsey slunk down. How could they have forgotten? She felt so ashamed. In the new quiet, she scanned the kitchen, painted what Dad called *puke* green, the only decoration, a copper "Bless This House" plaque, which hung over the stove, a present for their 10th anniversary.

The kitchen didn't even contain a ticking clock, something to listen to the seconds pass away. Digital clocks glowed from the oven and the microwave, each set to a different time: 6:05 and 6:07. The wait seemed endless. Would Dad ever come down and tell them what was going on or, maybe worse or then again maybe not worse, continue his yelling?

At that, Aunt Angie burst in through the back door, whipping in a cold wind. "I got here as soon as I could." She stomped her feet on the braided rag rug that lay in front of the door and stepped up into the kitchen, a ghost rising out of the night in a pale blue winter coat and hat. She threw her coat across one of the empty kitchen chairs and dropped a black leather bag on the floor.

The coat fell into a soft pile, like the sweaters at Lacy's that Lindsey had run her hands across when she'd rushed from the store to PetFarm. Could a coat be made of cashmere? As if reading her thoughts, Aunt Angie arranged her coat on the chair with more care, and took off her black leather gloves and laid them on top. She patted her short blonde hair. Before she'd married Uncle Marv last year, Aunt Angie's brown roots had always showed, making her hair seem like candy corn, half brown and half dyed blonde. Now, Aunt Angie's hair was always freshly dyed blonde with no roots, and her face and body were wrinkle- and fat-free.

"Ellen?" Aunt Angie called. "Sis? Where are you?"

"Shh," Jenna said, from where she sat at the table. "Dad's with her. It's a bad karma day."

"Oh, honey, I'm so sorry." Aunt Angie threw her arms out. "Come give me a hug."

Jenna shook her head. "We can't move; we're mentally and physically grounded. We fought at the store."

Aunt Angie placed her hand on her heart. "I'm ashamed of you. Fighting when your mother fainted, why, it's—it's—unseemly."

"Gwen wouldn't let me do what I wanted to do," Jenna said. "Which was the right thing." She stuck her tongue at Gwen. "And Lindsey wouldn't stand up to her." She stuck her tongue at Lindsey.

"Aunt Angie, let me explain." Gwen tapped her finger on the table. "You know how childish, really juvenile she is." Gwen titled her head toward Jenna. "Under these circumstances." She tapped her finger again. "These specific circumstances, we needed a longer time than the button would have allowed." With one last tap, Gwen finished. "I made the right decision."

Jenna stuck her tongue out again.

"Now, Jenna." Aunt Angie hugged Jenna from around the kitchen chair. "I brought you something." She reached in her bag and passed Jenna a brown and black plush dachshund puppy over her head. "Since you can't have a real puppy—yet." Aunt Angie smiled at Lindsey.

"It's beautiful." Jenna patted its short stiff hair and shivered. "Lindsey, you see." Jenna slid the dog across the kitchen table to Lindsey. Lindsey touched it but jumped back. The dog breathed in and out as if real.

"Isn't it great?" Aunt Angie laughed. "It's the latest thing in stuffed animals. They breathe."

"I don't know." Lindsey pushed her hair behind her ear. "Maybe it's kind of creepy." Then she pulled her hair forward and added, "I don't know," so she wouldn't hurt Aunt Angie's feelings. She slid the dog to Gwen.

Gwen inspected it. "It's called the Uncanny Valley. Why you hate this dog."

"Gwen!" Aunt Angie frowned, but her forehead stayed smooth.

"I'm stating a fact. It's too real." Gwen slid it back to Jenna, who let it sit where it was, an abandoned puppy.

"Besides, Aunt Angie," Jenna said. "You know that Lindsey and I want a Yorkshire Terrier."

"Oh, Jenna. Don't be silly. Dachshunds are the most popular dog right now. Yorkshire Terriers are so yesterday."

"But I love yesterday! Elizabeth Taylor had a Yorkshire Terrier. And we want a Yorkshire Terrier, don't we, Lindsey?"

Lindsey shrugged. All she needed was to hurt Aunt Angie's feelings again, but a dachshund was one ugly dog. That she did know.

"How can you possibly know who Elizabeth Taylor is?" Aunt Angie asked.

"Don't know Elizabeth Taylor? How can you say that?" Jenna tilted her chair back. "Of course I do. She's in *Lassie Come Home*, and *A Date with Judy*." Jenna counted on her fingers. "And, those aren't even black and white. For black and white, she's in *Father of the Bride*, and—"

"Alright, Alright. I forgot about your obsession with movies. But to me it proves again that little girls don't know what they want." Aunt Angie slid the new headband from Jenna's hair, and shaped her long hair into a ponytail with her hands. "You should wear this string of hair in a ponytail or a topknot. It would appear fuller. Why don't you get me the furball scrunchie I got you, and let me fix it?"

"I can't get up, remember?" Jenna twisted her hair free of Aunt Angie. She smoothed her hair into a straight line behind her back, the way Lindsey knew she liked it.

"Have you girls eaten? Gwen, how about ordering pizza? I'll buy so get whatever you want; something fancy, even sardines." Aunt Angie handed Gwen her smart phone. Gwen took it as if she was hungry for the phone and not pizza—Dad had cancelled their service and now they had only plain phones.

Gwen swiped the screen. "OK if I text Lauren, first?" Without waiting for an answer, she started texting. Lindsey leaned in to watch, and Gwen clasped her hand over the phone. "Cheat." Lindsey pulled back.

"Pizza!" Jenna shouted. "I've been like positively *dying* for pizza. We never get to order it. But no sardines!" She shook her head and her black hair didn't even move. "Once Gwen ordered sardines and pineapple. She'd read it in some dumb intellectual book about beatniks who lived long ago."

"Have Lindsey decide what's on it, then." Aunt Angie smiled at Lindsey.

"That's funny, Aunt Angie," Jenna said, and snorted. "Have Lindsey decide. We wouldn't eat."

"Yeah." Gwen said still texting. "She couldn't decide what makeup to buy either. You can still see the purple mess on her eyes."

"Oh, Lindsey," Aunt Angie said. "You didn't buy makeup? I gave you the money just for that. You're a teenager now. You're ordinary without it."

"I almost did. I mean." Lindsey rubbed her eyelids. "Is it gone?"

Jenna shook her head. "Negative."

Lindsey rubbed it again hoping she wasn't causing wrinkles. "I would have gone back, but we had to go home because Mom ..." At the thought of why, Lindsey stopped and so did everyone else. They waited while Gwen ordered the pizza, getting what she wanted as always.

"I'll bring you a cup a tea," Dad called and clambered down the stairs. He rounded the corner into the kitchen, stopping right before he crashed into Aunt Angie. He frowned and said, "Oh, hi, Angie. Ellen will be glad you're here. I'm getting her a cup of tea."

He hiked up his pants and tucked in his shirt as if he was falling apart from whatever was wrong. He hadn't changed from work and still wore his khakis and white shirt. His short red hair was as messy as short hair could be—tufts of it stuck together like cliques at a party.

"You don't need to bother making tea, Joe." Aunt Angie dug in her black bag and handed him a shiny purple thermos with a black knob on the top. "I brewed my special blend of chamomile from *Tea for Two* to perfection for her."

"Thanks." Dad took the thermos and tossed it back and forth in his hands like a bad juggler. "I'll start tacos for dinner then. Are you staying?"

"I had Gwennie order pizza. I'm paying *and* staying. Marv is working late so I can stay—well, all night!"

"Oh, great." Dad wrinkled his nose like something smelled. "I can always count on you, Angie."

"Of course. I won't let you down." She squeezed Dad's shoulder.

"Yes, well." Dad stood by the cupboards. Lindsey guessed that Aunt Angie had stopped Dad from both cooking and yelling. Both things were good to stop. Dad liked to experiment—once he added Coca Cola to rice and mixed bratwurst into meatloaf—everything had to be an invention. Even pizza with a wild Gwen-designed concoction would be better than that.

Mom shuffled around the corner holding on to the wall and dragging a brown fleece blanket speckled with pictures of footballs behind her. She looked more like a curly-haired Jenna than a mom. Gwen rushed to hold up the blanket and direct her to the table.

Aunt Angie pulled out a chair for her. "Are you sure you're OK to come down?"

"I'm fine now." Mom sagged into the chair, the fleece blanket falling to the floor. "Going shopping after work with the girls was too much."

Mom's dark curls stood stark against her white face. Lindsey wondered if she should do something for her—grab the blanket and wrap it tight around her or maybe get her yellow sweater—the one Mom always wore when she felt sad—what Mom called her droops. But before she could decide, Gwen grabbed the yellow sweater from the hook by the back door and laid it across Mom's shoulders. She wrapped the fleece blanket around her legs. Aunt Angie smiled and patted Gwen's hand. Lindsey's conscience knocked her in the head. Why couldn't she ever *do* something?

"Thanks, Gwen." Mom pulled the blanket tighter. "When I heard you were here, Angie, I came down because I thought we could discuss things."

What did she have to discuss with Aunt Angie? Did it have to do with that decision Mom and Dad had been talking about at the store? Now that she was about to learn what was going on, Lindsey didn't want to hear. She sensed it was bad—deeply bad or they wouldn't act so fake. Where was her book? She was reading the latest in the Tamera series—a new one didn't come out again until Christmas. The heroine of the series, Tamera, was so confident. She commanded the halls of her high school, even taking her dog to school, a Yorkshire Terrier. That's what she'd do. Read her book. Lindsey stood and backed away, to her room and freedom and dreams of being who she wasn't. Before she got to the hall, Aunt Angie said something that stopped her.

"Oh, there's no need for further discussion. I've got it all planned. The girls will live with me."

At that moment, Aunt Cassie burst in.

"I'm here!" She wore a purple plaid raincoat, unbuttoned and held together with an orange belt. She'd wrapped her hair in a brown scarf, as if she'd only woken up even though Lindsey knew she'd worked all day at Jack and Jill's Daycare. "So you told them? That they're staying with me? I'm so excited." She tripped on the braided rug by the door and knocked her shins on the step as she stumbled into the kitchen. She took off her raincoat to reveal a red dress with a large black stain shaped like a blimp over her so

MORE WAITING

Lindsey stared at Jenna, who then stared at Gwen, who then stared back to Lindsey. What was going on? Were their parents sending them away? Like people who drop off their kids at a youth shelter because they couldn't deal with them, couldn't feed them? But they weren't that poor, were they? Lots of people had worn-out chairs, baggy carpeting, and filed for bankruptcy. Dad had just gotten a regular job, too, no more working for himself. Lindsey shook her head, whipping her hair in Gwen's face. Gwen didn't even scream at her.

"We're having a baby sister, is that it?" Jenna slid off her chair and stepped over to Mom to pat her stomach. "That's good news. You don't have to send us away like we're in some old movie. I, for one, would like a baby brother."

"No, Jenna." Mom hugged her. "No babies. Come here, girls. Come sit around me."

Lindsey shook her head and stayed near the hall—in case she needed to escape. Gwen took the opportunity to act all good and sickly sweet by sitting at Mom's feet and putting her head in her lap. Jenna shoved Gwen over a little to sit on Mom's lap too. Dad stood like a statue next to Aunt Cassie, while Aunt Angie sat next to Mom and held her hand.

"Dad and I were going to tell you later, but because of this afternoon we need to tell you now. I'm sick, girls, and it will take a lot to get me better."

"Oh, dear, are your headaches back?" Jenna rubbed Mom's temples. "Poor Momster. Remember when I did this when I was little? You wouldn't let me get your migraine medicine then, but I can now." She slid off Mom's lap and headed toward the cupboard.

"No, Jenna, honey, come back. I'm sicker than that. Come back."

Jenna returned with the aspirin bottle. "No migraine medicine, but two of these should help." Jenna handed it to Mom. "How many do you want?"

"Give me another hug, honey," Mom said. "That's what I want. You're making me cry. This isn't a sickness that aspirin would help. I've …" A sob escaped her again, and she held a balled-up tissue in front of her mouth and didn't continue. Lindsey and her family waited like sunflowers for the sun.

After a moment, Dad said, "I'll tell them, honey, you don't have to. Your mom, your mom …" He stopped too, swallowing so hard his Adam's apple bounced in his throat.

"I'll do it." Aunt Angie rose and cleared her throat. "Your mom, girls, has cancer. It's called non-Hodgkin lymphoma."

Lindsey screwed up her face. She'd never heard of that. Everyone always talked about breast cancer, and wore ribbons and everything. How many cancers were there?

"What? What did you say?" Jenna asked. "Non-who? Lindsey, what does that mean?" Jenna ran over to Lindsey. "It must mean it belongs to someone else, right, Lindsey? To someone who is not Hod—Hod—whatever." Lindsey didn't know how to respond so Jenna ran over to Dad. "Right, Daddy?" Dad stooped to talk to Jenna eye to eye. He placed his hands on her shoulders.

"Jenna, listen," he said. "It's a name of a doctor, Hodgkin, who studied cancers. If they didn't fit into his categories, he called them non-Hodgkin."

"Well, I *hate* him and he shouldn't have discovered it and Mom shouldn't be sick with it," she cried. Dad picked her up. She was so long and skinny that she was only a foot off of the ground. "I don't want her to be sick," she sobbed into his shoulder.

Lindsey felt her throat thicken with sadness. She studied her aunts. Their heads both tilted to the right, and they frowned like they felt sorry for her family. She didn't want people feeling sorry for them, pitying them. People usually did when they saw their worn-out house and car and Dad's inventions in the garage.

"Jenna, it'll be alright." Mom stood to pat Jenna on the back. "I'll get better. I have stage 2. Dad's going to take care of me. He'll drive me to the hospital; help me throw up." She stopped, not even smiling at her almost joke. She continued, "The cancer medicine makes you pretty sick."

"Those doctors are horrible," Jenna said. "To make you sicker. It doesn't make any sense."

"Oh, come on," Lindsey said in response to Jenna. Everyone frowned at her. "Sorry." She did feel sorry for Jenna, but why did she need to act like a baby?

"That's how the chemo works," Dad said. "It kills the cancer cells but sometimes it gets the good ones, too."

Lindsey realized that Gwen hadn't said anything, hadn't commented that she already knew about non-Hodgkin, had studied it in depth on Wikipedia, could recite the statistics, or the survival rate. Instead, she sat with her hands folded in her lap and her eyes cast down, watching her hands as if they might run away.

Run away! She should have left before and never heard the news. But now that she had, she'd figure this out by herself in her room, with her books, wrapped in a blanket. She backed away, a thief stooping out of sight, but Aunt Angie's arm blocked her escape and her aunt's green-flecked eyes stormed at her. Lindsey slumped into a chair. What business was it of Aunt Angie's if she left?

"Your dad will have to work and help me at the same time," Mom was saying. "It's a big undertaking. That's why we decided that you girls should live with one of your aunts."

"Will he get fired?" Jenna asked.

"No, he'll have to balance work and home because he just started. We can't afford to lose this job or we lose the health insurance to pay for my medicine." Mom stopped talking and looked out the window at the bleak November wind blowing and whipping the trees. Dad put Jenna down and wrapped his arm around Mom. Aunt Angie pulled Jenna toward her, while Aunt Cassie trotted to the bathroom and returned with a box of tissues. "Dig in everyone."

Her family pulled tissues from the box and cried, including Dad. How horrible. She wanted to cry too, and her throat held a rock. But she wouldn't cry in front of everyone. She'd hold it together. She sniffed, and grabbed a tissue. Deep sadness overwhelmed her like tiredness and a cry erupted from her. She placed her hand over her mouth to stop it, but more flooded out, from deep inside her poor sad heart—she didn't know it could hurt so bad or she could cry so much.

A few minutes later, the doorbell rang.

"Enough." Aunt Angie blew into her soggy tissue. "Your mom's going to be fine."

Mom searched Dad's face as if pleading that he believed it too.

"Besides, we don't want soggy pizza. Here, Cassie, take the money for the pizza." Aunt Angie forced a $20 bill into Aunt Cassie's hands. "Give it to the boy, will you?"

"For Pete's sake, Ang!" Aunt Cassie let the money drop to the floor. "You ordered it. You open the door and pay him." Aunt Angie picked up the dollar and like a queen awaiting her subjects, stepped down to open the door.

"Aunt Angie's right," Mom said, while Aunt Angie exchanged pleasantries with the pizza guy and Dad set the table. "Silly of me to cry. And, you too, Jenna and you, Lindsey, and Gwen. Everything will be fine after the chemo and radiation."

"Radiation!" Jenna sobbed into her hands. "You have to do that too?"

"Now, honey." Mom patted Jenna's head. "That's how you get well."

Aunt Angie returned with a grease-stained Bob's Better Pizza box. "Sit down everyone, and dig in." She inhaled. "Smells great, although Uncle Marv and I usually have François, our cook, make it for us. I never knew how good pizza could be when it was homemade. Wunderbar." Aunt Angie lifted the pizza lid, uncovering a pizza littered with ham, sausage, and pepperoni. "Oops, sorry, Cassie. Gwen ordered meat toppings. Terrible mistake. Now you can't eat any, which might be chance to lose a pound."

"Don't worry about me, Angie." Aunt Cassie reached for a slice and dropped it on her plate. "I can make do." She picked off a piece of ham and placed in on her plate. "It's all about the girls." She singled out a sausage and laid it next to the ham, arranging the sausage and ham so they were parallel "Yes, indeed." She sighed and scooped out a pepperoni half buried in the cheese, and set it next to the sausage. Lindsey imagined waking up in the morning and finding Aunt Cassie still there—plucking a sausage, lifting a pepperoni, picking a ham …

"Sorry, Aunt Cassie," Gwen said.

Aunt Cassie patted Gwen's hand with her grease-stained fingers.

"It might be better if you used a fork." Gwen got up to fetch her one.

Aunt Angie bit into her slice, tearing off a chunk. She chewed and asked, "So who's going to live with me?" She stopped to swallow. "You will, won't you, Jenna?" Aunt Angie tugged Jenna toward her. Jenna juggled her pizza to keep it from falling. "Wouldn't you like that? I'd buy you lots of pretty things."

"But you can live with me, too, Jenna." Aunt Cassie tugged Jenna toward her, making Jenna's pizza fall meat-side down. Aunt Cassie picked it up and began putting meat back *on* the pizza, first the sausage, then the ham … She continued talking. "We can have lots of fun, you and me, doing crazy things with my dogs and cats." Aunt Cassie had smashed Jenna into the black stain on her dress. Could it be gross kid stuff from the preschool? Lindsey shivered.

Lindsey listened to her aunts persuade Jenna to live with them. Would they fight to have *her* live with them? She both wanted them to fight over her and leave her alone. But the aunts stopped persuading Jenna and returned to their favorite subject, each other.

"You work, Cassie. I don't." Aunt Angie scooted her chair closer to Aunt Cassie's. "So I'll always be available for the girls. And the girls need a father figure, like my Marv."

"Since I work at a daycare," Aunt Cassie answered, scooting her chair away. "I only work while they're at school. And they already have a father so they don't need a father figure. What are you trying to do, Ang, make up for the lack of a family in your own life?"

"Oh, that was low," Aunt Angie replied. "Really low. It's not like you have such a wonderful life. Working at a low-paying job, taking care of kids whose parents drop them off and don't want to see them again until evening."

"OK, OK," Dad hovered his hand over the table as if he wanted to slam it down. "Enough. You both have good qualifications. If you're going to fight about it, Ellen and I'll decide for the girls."

"Oh, we don't want that," Aunt Angie said. "It'll be healthier for the girls to decide."

"So, girls, who will it be?" Aunt Cassie sat back and clasped her hands around her black stain. "You can't wait much longer. Your mom starts chemo on Monday."

Lindsey's eyes met Gwen's. She could tell they were thinking the same thing. How could they make a decision in front of the aunts? Besides, Lindsey didn't want to make a decision at all. How could she? It would be great to live with Aunt Angie. Imagine all the stuff she would buy. But then think of Aunt Cassie. Crazy Aunt Cassie with her cherry red VW beetle, argyle socks, and plaid coat. She'd take them places they'd never been before, like the Farmer's Market and the cheese factory, and she'd let them stay up as long as they wanted.

But she really didn't want to live with either of them. She wanted to stay home with Mom. Do all the things she could to help: serve Mom a cup of tea, fetch her medicine, read her a book. But she knew she'd be afraid and freeze. Afraid she'd make the tea too hot, drop the pills on the floor, and mispronounce all the words. Maybe she should accept her fate so she asked:

"How long do we have to live with, you know, someone else?"

"Well." Dad scratched his nose. "That depends." He pulled on his ear. "It might be six weeks." He hiked up his pants. "But more likely three months." He sighed. "Or as many as six."

Six months! What would it be like to not be in your own bed for six months? Not watch your own T.V. and lay around in your pajamas until noon? Aunt Cassie would have them up at the Farmer's market by 8:00 on Saturdays. Aunt Angie would take them to lunch at the art museum and quiz them on the art before allowing them to take a bite. It was too awful to imagine.

"Stay with me, girls." Aunt Cassie held out her arms. "Come here, Lindsey, Gwen. A hug for Aunt Cassie." Oh, brother, thought Lindsey, but before she moved, Aunt Angie said:

"Cassie! That's not fair. Girls, come to your Aunt Angie." A touch of sadness crept into her voice. Was Aunt Angie as lonely as Aunt Cassie said she was?

"OK, that's enough, Angie." Aunt Cassie pressed her hands to the sides of her head. "How can they decide in this tug of war? The girls need time to think. They've only learned about Ellen and now they have to decide where to live. Life's got them over a barrel. They need space to make a decision."

"How about a girl's weekend away?" Mom swiped her hair behind her ear only to have it pop back. "We've always dreamed of one, but what with Joe's business and school and church and things, we never did."

"Maybe now's the time." Dad put his arm around Mom.

"Oh, but Joe," Mom said, her eyes wide and liquid. "We don't have the money. The chemo, the radiation, the bills."

"This is not the time to think about money," he replied squeezing Mom even tighter.

"Funny *you* should say that." Aunt Angie pointed at Dad. He dropped his arm from around Mom. "If you hadn't spent all your savings on that cockamamie idea of yours out in the garage, imagine what you could give Ellen and the girls. Marv told you it wouldn't work. *You* run a business." Aunt Angie threw out her chest.

Jenna stood up, placing her hands on her hips that were so narrow her hands slid down. "Don't say that. My dad's idea was great. He would never hurt my mother."

Dad patted Jenna's head. "It's OK, Jenna. Aunt Angie's angry and she likes to use me for the reason. And maybe she's right. Maybe if I named my invention Cockamamie, Inc., it would have worked. But that's behind us now, Angie. Don't say things you'll regret and don't mean."

Aunt Angie sniffed and jabbed a pepperoni deep into the hardened cheese of the leftover pizza.

"So, Jenna," Dad said. "Do you want to have fun before you make your decision? Where would you want to go? Hollywood?"

Jenna moved forward to answer him but he continued.

"What about you, Linds? The library? Or Paris for you, Gwennie?" He winked. Lindsey felt all mushy inside whenever Dad winked at her. He could wrinkle up one eye and pour a gallon of love into the other. Could she survive six months without a wink?

"Joe." Mom shook her head. "Please don't fill their heads with dreams."

"Like he did with yours?" Aunt Angie snorted and then looked a bit sorry. "Seriously, Marv has a timeshare. It's short notice, and there may be an extra fee, but I don't mind. Come on, Gwen, let's see what's available."

Gwen and Aunt Angie headed to the computer in the living room with Aunt Angie's arm tucked around Gwen's. Lindsey cringed at Aunt Angie snooping at the papers surrounding the computer that sat in the corner of their living room, where Dad had worked on business and which now had all their bills and bankruptcy papers strewn about.

"It has to be in driving distance," Mom called after them. "Let's keep it practical."

"Listen, Ellen. You don't need a timeshare." Aunt Cassie moved to sit next to Mom in Aunt Angie's vacated chair. "That's so wasteful and impersonal. Stay at my friend's organic farm. It's about 20 or so miles from here. It would do you good, Ellen. Drinking the rich raw milk and eating the fresh local vegetables. The earth would heal you."

Lindsey shrank back in horror. Drink raw milk! Didn't you get diseases from that? After all, it was *illegal!* Aunt Cassie better not feed it to them if they lived with her.

"Stop! Stop!" Jenna waved her arms and jumped up and down. "You guys aren't listening. I already know the solution. We don't have to go to Hollywood or Paris or an organic farm. We can go to Niagara Falls. Lindsey says there is a museum there with wax statues of famous people. That's where I want to go. Lindsey too."

"Niagara Falls?" Aunt Angie hurried in from the living room and stood in the kitchen doorway. "That's one lousy tourist trap. Positively trash. I'm sure Lindsey would rather go somewhere more sophisticated than that, right, Lindsey?"

"I, I don't know," Lindsey felt her mouth go dry so she added, "Maybe."

"Lindsey!" Jenna thumped Lindsey's shoulder.

"Ouch!" Lindsey let her shoulder sag.

"Oh, don't be a baby. You want to go. You know you do. It's our dream. Lindsey's been reading about it for days and days, about the lady who went over the Falls in a barrel, Annie Edison somebody." Jenna tiptoed to Aunt Angie. "She padded the barrel with a mattress and survived! She's a daredevil. That's why Lindsey likes her."

"Jenna." Lindsey shook her head. She should know better than to tell Jenna her secrets. They'd been researching wax museums on Wikipedia when they'd clicked a link about a lady going over Niagara Falls in a barrel—Annie Taylor Edison. But Jenna was right. The lady was pretty cool, and old. Sixty-three!

"Well, I'm sure Gwen would rather go somewhere else." Aunt Angie called back to Gwen in the living room. "Gwen, where would you like to go?"

Gwen appeared behind Aunt Angie. "Unless I can see Paris, everything else is mediocre. The mediocre principle doesn't apply to Paris." Gwen stopped and waited for a response. "Don't you get it? It's a joke, guys. The mediocre principle? Oh, bother. Well, anyway, I'd go because they might speak French since Niagara Falls is in Canada. I mean, maybe it'd be OK." Gwen returned to the computer.

"See, Aunt Angie." Jenna twirled around. "We're all dreaming of it. And, best of all, there is a Festival of Lights in November. Lights, Aunt Angie!" Jenna threw her arms up in the air. "Lights everywhere! It'll be heaven."

"So you want to go to that horrible tourist trap?" Aunt Angie asked. "What if you fall in?"

"Now, *you're* being childish." Jenna folded her arms and smiled.

"Niagara Falls." Dad rubbed his stomach, which Lindsey thought of as his nice pouch. "We used to go there when I was a kid. I always liked the surging rush of the water and the blue raincoats you wore when you went under the Falls. I always imagined I'd invent an underwater submersible to go under the Falls." Dad dove his hand under the table mimicking a submarine. "I still could do it, right, Lindsey?"

Lindsey nodded. Of course he could.

"Oh, remember, Ellen and Ang." Aunt Cassie raised both her hands. "The summer we went to the Falls when we were kids? We bought ice cream cones and you ate your chocolate so slowly, Ang, because you wanted yours to last longer than ours and it melted all over your new white dress." Aunt Cassie gestured to her own spotted dress. "Dad was so mad when he had to drag you back to the hotel and there was no time to go under the Falls in the Maid of the Mist. You should have seen her, Lindsey."

Aunt Cassie laughed and Aunt Angie frowned and crinkled her forehead.

"Don't frown, Ang, or Marv will have to buy you more Botox." Aunt Cassie laughed and laughed, bending over the table near Jenna's scratch.

Mom tapped Cassie gently on the arm. "Now, that's mean, Cassie." Aunt Cassie stopped and pouted like Jenna.

Gwen called from the living room where the old computer monitor glowed on her face. "I mapped it. It's a five-hour car ride. There's also a condo available at the Hotel Grandeur."

"Sounds like good karma to me." Jenna twirled around the table, and then stopped. "Hotel Grandeur sounds exotic. I bet celebrities stay there. Maybe we'll meet tons in the lobby."

Aunt Cassie came alive from her pout and cried, "I'll drive you."

"What? In your itty bitty beetle as big as the space between my fingers." Aunt Angie pinched her fingers together. "The girls would fall out."

"Well, it beats your mega-ton SUV," Aunt Cassie replied. "So big, it's like you're a turtle carrying a humongous shell, with exhaust erupting from it and polluting the Earth. And I wasn't going to drive them in my car. I was going to drive them in *theirs*."

"I'm not sure theirs is much better than yours. No offense, Joe, but it needs a sign, Watch for Falling Parts." Aunt Angie smiled as she said this, but no one smiled back. "I guess I'll save the day again." Aunt Angie pressed the tips of her fingers together. "I'll rent you a limousine and chauffeur for the weekend. That way neither of us has an unfair advantage."

"Yeah!" Jenna yelled. "Our dream is coming true!"

For once, Lindsey agreed with all her heart.

PACKING UP PINK

Forty-eight hours later, Mom's faded pink suitcase from college lay open on Lindsey's bed. It had a hard outer casing and closed with a lock. Clothes erupted out of it, some buried in her rumpled purple bed sheets. Lindsey yawned. She was supposed to have cleaned her room and packed, but she'd done neither. How could someone be expected to do all that when that someone needed to read two chapters of Tamera's adventures before getting up?

Lindsey shared a room with Jenna. Their sides of the room were identical, except for the impeccable neatness of Jenna's side and for it being overstuffed with stuffed animals—brown teddy bears, shaggy green frogs, dinosaurs, and on top of the entire pile, a fluffy white poodle.

Jenna and Lindsey each had a bed with a white headboard but shared a single orange chest of drawers that had been Aunt Cassie's and Mom's. Lindsey never failed to read the words, "*I hate Miss Kurtz,*" that Mom had scratched into the front of the top drawer with a hat pin. They'd painted over it but it was persistent—tenacious, as Gwen liked to say—Mom's hatred of her third grade teacher living forever.

Lindsey lifted a pink sweater from her messy bed and studied it. It buttoned down the front with pearl buttons and pink lace. It was Gwen's, but Lindsey looked good in pink. The purple eye shadow might have looked good with it too.

Lindsey pursed her lips. Maybe Gwen wouldn't notice if she wore it, as long as she kept her jacket on. After all, Gwen had already packed and she hadn't taken it. Lindsey tugged it on over her white turtleneck. It would look good with that, too. She had to wear it. It was meant to be, good karma.

Jenna walked in with Gwen. "Gwen's helping me pack, but I don't need any help. I know what to take. Everybody in!" Jenna threw her favorite teddy bear, the shaggy frog, and finally her poodle into a round white suitcase that Aunt Angie had given her. The poodle wouldn't fit, so she tossed it on to her bed. "I'll carry you. I know I'm supposed to be too old for them, but somehow I need them this weekend." She sprinted back to the dresser and yanked open the top drawer. She grabbed a pile of underwear and threw them in her suitcase.

Jenna glanced at Lindsey. "Why aren't you packing, Lindsey?"

"Oh, I don't know." Lindsey wrapped her arms around herself so Gwen wouldn't notice the sweater. She didn't have to though because Gwen was too busy taking out the items in the suitcase that Jenna had so busily put in. "I can't decide what to take."

"Did you do what I told you to do?" Gwen looked over at Lindsey. "Make a list. Check the weather. Find an outfit for each planned activity. I printed copies of the activity list for each of you."

Lindsey picked up her list from the bed. "Yes, I've got the list." She concentrated on the mess of clothes. What should she take? She lifted a blouse and sniffed it. She wasn't even sure if any of her clothes were clean.

"You're so helpless," Gwen said. "With everything else I have to do, I guess I have to pack for you too."

"You go ahead and help her, Gwen." Jenna pulled a pink checked summer dress from the closet and shoved the dress, hanger and all, into her suitcase. "I don't need any help. I know what to take."

Gwen inspected Lindsey's suitcase. To hide the sweater, Lindsey skidded over to Jenna's bed and slid under the tower of stuffed animals, brushing a purple brontosaur's tail from her face. Another gift from Aunt Angie on Jenna's third birthday.

Gwen yanked a silky white top free from Lindsey's suitcase. "This is a summer top. Really, you should know better. You're as illogical as Jenna." Gwen threw the top on the bed. She rooted around in the suitcase.

"Hey! There's something hard in here. What are these?" Gwen pulled a library book from underneath Lindsey's pajamas. She read the title, "*For the Love of Boys!*" She stuck her hand in and pulled out another, "*Love is Forever*," and another, "*High School Loves*," and finally, "*Celebrity Dogs*."

"Celebrity Dogs?"

She threw them all on the bed. Lindsey slid across the floor in her socks, grabbed the books, and hid them behind her back. Thankfully, Gwen wasn't as observant as she prided herself on being because besides not noticing the sweater, she hadn't noticed the biography—a picture book called *Annie's Antics* about Annie Edison Taylor who'd gone over the Falls in a barrel. What a relief. She didn't want Gwen ridiculing her all weekend.

"This stuff's junk," Gwen lectured. "You should be reading serious stuff, like books on the economy, and Mom's …, Mom's …, well, you know. Besides, we won't have time for reading. We're going to have fun. You saw the list. Wax museum, Niagara Falls. Lights. Choirs singing Christmas carols. Fun. It may be the last fun we have."

"Stop it." Lindsey shoved the books back down around the sides of the suitcase. "You're scaring me. Besides, I like them all, and I couldn't decide which one to bring." She shut the suitcase, but it bounced back open. She shut it again, and before it could pop open, she sat on it, only to totter over on the bed.

Lindsey climbed back on the suitcase. "Hold me up, Gwen." Clothes oozed out like cream. She tugged on the latch, but it wouldn't lock.

"Whatever." Gwen faced the door. "I've lost my patience. I know you're going to stick your nose in those books and not make your decision and let the aunts and everybody run all over you. They're out there, you know, waiting to say goodbye. They've got presents too."

"Presents!" Jenna yelled. "I'm getting mine." She skipped out with Gwen, her suitcase, and poodle.

Whew, that was close. Gwen hadn't noticed the sweater or the book. She was lucky but she felt uncomfortable, as if someone watched her. She glanced up. Gwen stood in the doorway.

"What are you wearing?" Gwen pronounced each word slowly and clearly, "What ... are ... you ..." Gwen's eyes beamed lasers at the sweater.

"Well, you didn't take it and it's perfect for visiting the museum." Lindsey smoothed the front of the sweater and finished buttoning it. "It fits the list, like you said."

"Funny how you're able to decide to bring," Gwen pinched the sleeve. "Something that doesn't belong to you—but to me."

"Ow." Lindsey yanked back. "You pinched *me*." Her blood boiled. She couldn't understand why so much anger bubbled up.

"It's *my* sweater and I'll pinch it if I want." Gwen tugged the collar. "Take it off."

"You're going to wreck it." Lindsey brushed Gwen's hands away. "You lent it to me once."

"Borrow once doesn't mean keep forever." Gwen's face lit up a bright red and she slapped Lindsey's arm.

Lindsey pushed her away. Gwen fell back and pulled Lindsey with her, tumbling into a pile of stuffed animals and books. Lindsey's elbow hit Gwen's head, sending a twinge up Lindsey's arm.

"Hey!" Gwen sprang up. "You want to fight for real?" She slammed a fist into Lindsey's arm. She pinched Lindsey's upper arm, digging her nails into the soft sweater and finger-nail deep into Lindsey's arm. "This time I meant to get you." Gwen's eyes formed beads as she shoved her nails into Lindsey.

"Ah!" Lindsey felt pain, yes, but mostly anger, a gazillion buckets of anger. Gwen who was always perfect, Gwen who could keep her cool so she won every fight. Well, not this time. Lindsey closed her eyes, clinched her fists, and punched at Gwen like a boxer, feeling nothing but air, but then, once, she felt something hard, and heard Gwen suck in. Had she actually hit her? As if in answer, Gwen yanked Lindsey's hair.

"Ow!" Lindsey clawed Gwen's arm.

"Doesn't bother me in the least, you creep." Gwen scratched back.

"Girls!" Aunt Angie yelled. "Girls! No wonder your mom can't get well!"

Lindsey stopped and opened her eyes. Mom scowled down at her like she said her hated teacher Mrs. Kurtz had, with the aunts standing behind like her minions.

"I'm only protecting my property." Gwen leaned her weight against Lindsey and rose. "I'll be ready in a sec, Mother. Lindsey stole my sweater."

Gwen held out her hand and Lindsey took off the sweater. She opened Lindsey's closet and hung it up, slamming the door shut with a decisive clap. If there'd been a lock, Gwen would have swallowed the key. "We can go now." Gwen patted her hair in the mirror, touching her blonde streak. She joined the aunts and Mom towering over Lindsey.

Lindsey stayed stuck where she was, her arms stinging from Gwen's pinches and slaps, surely bleeding profusely. She inspected her arms. Nothing on the outside but she knew, and felt, that on the inside, she was bleeding gushers.

"I'm so disappointed in you, Lindsey." Mom wiped a tear away, and left, with the aunts and Gwen following.

Lindsey eyes welled up. Mom was disappointed in her? Why only her? Gwen had started it. Lindsey had only defended herself—stuck up for herself like everyone told her too. *"Lindsey, Gwen always walks all over you, don't let her." "Lindsey, tell her what you want."* Hadn't she been doing that?

The front door slammed shut and silence invaded the house. Everyone had gone. Good. What did she care? She'd stay here. Dad wouldn't notice. He'd probably work all night on his inventions—inventions that he promised to give up. She'd be alone, which would be a dream come true. To read long into the night until her eyes blurred. To stuff herself with cupcakes, chips, and all the junk food in the cupboards. What did she care about Niagara Falls? About the limousine? The museum?

Creak!

Lindsey jumped. What was that? She shrugged. It didn't bother her. Noises couldn't budge her. She pulled her books out of her suitcase and studied the picture book about Annie Edison Taylor. The cover showed the water rushing down the Falls, all foam and mist. Seeing it on the cover was good enough. She didn't need to feel its power or sting. She'd read about it.

Bang!

All alone. With no one. Just strange, creepy noises.

Crash!

Yes, fine to be alone in this lonely, haunted house.

Creak! Bang!

Lindsey leapt up. "Don't go without me!" She ran to the closet and yanked the sweater off the hanger. She threw it in her suitcase, shoved the books back in the sides, and squished the suitcase shut. Oh, no! She wasn't wearing shoes. What to wear? She slipped on a pair and ran out.

LEAVING IN STYLE

Out on the driveway, Jenna leaned against their white station wagon picking rust off of a fender.

"Oh, Lindsey. You came. Gwen said you weren't."

"Did I?" Gwen called from where she stood at the end of the driveway with Mom and the aunts searching for the limousine. "I try not to focus on her or her juvenile delinquent behavior."

Lindsey joined Jenna, not wanting Mom or the aunts to notice her. She shivered in her gray coat, her driveway filled only with cold and wind, the sun fighting through more November clouds and losing.

Next door, Mrs. Smythe peeked out her kitchen window, and across the street, the Browns sat on their porch, their jacket collars tucked tight around them. They probably wanted to see another company arrive to carry off more of their stuff from the bankruptcy. Wouldn't they be surprised when a limousine drove up? A thrill ran through her. A limousine for *them*!

"How does my new hat look?" Jenna touched a floppy pink and red polka dotted hippy hat she wore.

"Ridiculous, utterly ridiculous." Gwen walked over and tried to take it off. "Mother, if she wears that, she'll embarrass us all."

"She likes it, Gwen. It's fine." Mom joined them. She pushed her hand through her hair and rubbed the back of her neck. Lindsey's heart ached to watch her. How strange to have an adventure because of Mom's sickness.

"And, I bought it for her." Aunt Cassie added herself to the group. She wore a crochet zebra-striped poncho. Nice Aunt Cassie. Lindsey could almost imagine living with her, but she wasn't sure she could stand the embarrassment of her outfits. What if she picked her up from school?

"And how do you like my high heels?" Jenna rotated her feet like a model.

"You'll fall," Gwen said.

"Jenna," Lindsey added. "You're going to be walking everywhere."

"I gave them to her, Gwen." Aunt Angie walked over too. She continued shielding her eyes, searching the horizon for the limousine. "I see it. The limo's here!" She rose up on her toes and pointed down the street.

A black limousine turned into their driveway, filling its entire length and hanging a bit into the street. An utter wow! Better than any limousine Tamera, the heroine of Lindsey's favorite books, had ridden in to her many proms. Fantastic!

A chauffeur emerged dressed all in black with a red stripe down each pant leg and a matching hat with a silver emblem. Aunt Angie greeted him and he touched his hat in salute, the emblem flashing even in the weak November sun. After a moment, the trunk opened smoothly and magically, the chauffeur not even holding a key fob. Lindsey shivered now, not from cold, but from excitement—and fear!

"Everyone, put your suitcases in," Aunt Angie called.

"May I take yours?" The chauffeur reached for Lindsey's suitcase but she shrugged and shoved hers in next to Jenna's. She didn't want the chauffeur to know it didn't shut. Besides, if it stayed pressed up against the others, nothing would fall out during the ride, especially One Pretty Pink Sweater Owed by One Evil Sister. Hey, that's OPPSOOES!

Jenna hugged Lindsey. "I'm so excited. I've never been in a limousine before. Duh."

Lindsey laughed and hugged her back. "Neither have I. Double duh." They jumped up and down and squealed. It felt good. Jenna always made her forget her troubles and enjoy the moment.

"Lindsey, stop it," Gwen ridiculed. "Childish again. The chauffeur is watching." Then, she added in a whisper, "Do you think he's married?"

"Not to you." Jenna laughed. "Nobody's going to marry stuck-up old you."

"No one's going to marry you either, miss skinny Minnie," Gwen retorted back.

"Why I'otta slug you." Jenna swung her arms around only to totter over in her high heels and fall.

Lindsey helped her up by her boney elbows. "Gwen, you made her fall!"

"I did? She's the one wearing high heels. Why do you always take her side?"

"Stop it, girls!" Dad had walked out of the garage to say goodbye. "Stop it now. Don't you understand that this behavior is why your mother is sending you away?"

"But Gwen shouldn't pick on us," Jenna said.

"Now, girls." Aunt Angie put her arm around Aunt Cassie. "Take us as an example." Aunt Cassie smiled like her feet hurt and then pulled away. Aunt Angie stepped over to stand besides Mom.

"Ellen, dear," she said. "Take this." She held out a roll of $20 bills as wide as a can of Coke. "You might need a little extra cash."

"No, Angie," Mom answered and Dad shook his head in agreement, wrapping his arms around Mom's waist and kissing her cheek. "You've done enough for us already. My, you rented such a large limousine." Mom raised her oversize tortoise-shell sunglasses and stared at the car and the chauffeur. Lindsey had sat on the sunglasses and warped them, but Mom wouldn't buy a new pair.

"Plenty of room for the girls so they won't fight. Well, enjoy the trip." Aunt Angie held out her arms. "Give me a hug, Lindsey." When Lindsey stepped forward, Aunt Angie pushed the money into Lindsey's hand.

Lindsey gasped, but Aunt Angie shushed her and said in a whisper, "Take care of your mom."

"Enjoy, girls." Aunt Cassie waved and squished herself into her VW. She backed up the car, and Aunt Angie ran to jump in. Lindsey heard them bicker as they drove away, "Cassie, you could have waited."

Lindsey turned back to her family and Dad saying, "I won't give you a speech. You know what's expected of you. Take care of your mother. Help out. Don't make her do everything."

The chauffeur opened the door for Mom. Lindsey peeked in to see two rows of seats in the back, everything awash in light grey. She inhaled the leathery smell that escaped. Fantastic again.

"Ready, ma'am?" he said. Wow, he'd called Mom, ma'am. Mom ducked in, holding the chauffeur's hand for support.

"Oh, my." Mom poked her head out of the window. "There's so much room in here. Angie's right. You girls won't have anything to fight over."

Jenna tugged on Lindsey's arm. "What do you want, Lindsey, to sit by the window or in the middle?"

Lindsey twisted her mouth. Window or middle? That was as bad as paper or plastic. Weren't there enough decisions?

Before she could speak, Gwen said, "I'll decide. You go in first Jenna so you're by the window." Gwen shoved Jenna in the limousine. "And you, Lindsey." She pulled Lindsey by the arm and into the limousine. "You sit in the middle. All you're going to do is read anyway."

Lindsey settled into her seat, pulling her jeans down around her ankles. She'd grown since they bought them for the first day of high school but Mom wouldn't buy her a new pair because "money was as tight as her jeans." Lindsey pushed the waist down. That was better. Another reason to live with Aunt Angie, for a new pair of jeans, and maybe the next book in the Tamera series, instead of 110th on the waiting list at the library.

She glanced around. Each of them had their own arm rests with plugs for computers, smart phones, and all other electronic gadgets imaginable, which of course, they didn't have. A DVD screen hung across from Mom's seat, and, what Lindsey cared most about, a light glowed over hers, like on an airplane. Oh, the reading she'd get done.

"I wonder what this does." Jenna pushed a button on her arm rest. The window between them and the driver opened.

"Is there something I can do for you?" The chauffeur's voice boomed through a speaker behind Lindsey and she jumped.

"Yes, indeed." Jenna raised her voice to a high pitch. "Is there a bathroom in here?" She adjusted her hippy hat.

Gwen hit her forehead with her hand. "Jenna, do you have to embarrass us *all* the time?"

"We're fine," Mom called to the chauffeur. "Please ignore the interruption. We're ready whenever you are." She closed the window between them. "Jenna, please don't play with that anymore."

"Alright. Alright." Jenna dug in her pocket of her coat and pulled out a scratched and battered DVD, without a case. "As soon as we get started, I'll put in my movie. It's *Bringing up Baby* with my favorite black-and-white movie star, Katherine Hepburn. I love Hollywood."

"Oh, that's so embarrassing too," Gwen said. "If it has to be black-and-white movie, couldn't it be a foreign film, preferably French?" Gwen pushed her hair back from her eyes. "I'm going to have a nervous breakdown before this weekend is over with these idiots and their choices."

"Let her be, Gwen." Mom settled back and put her head on the headrest. "Do you girls want to drive straight through or stop at a restaurant?" She removed her sunglasses revealing her beautiful eyes rimmed in red with dark blue shadows underneath. Now Lindsey knew why she'd wore them even in the weak November sun. "If we go straight through then we can have lunch in Niagara Falls. We can have only one meal out, though."

Lindsey felt liked grumbling and asking Mom why she hadn't taken the money from Aunt Angie if they didn't even have enough money for food, but her stomach grumbled for her. Breakfast, it said, yum, pancakes and bacon. But wait, what about lunch—hamburgers and French fries?

"Breakfast." Jenna smiled and rubbed Lindsey's arm. "You want breakfast, don't you, Lindsey?"

"Sure, yeah, OK." Lindsey smiled at Jenna and opened her book, *Tamera's Date*, and adjusted her light. Jenna may have answered awfully fast, but at least it meant she didn't have to decide.

"Mom, I mapped out all the restaurants along the way," Gwen said. "A French restaurant called Chez Café is about an hour away off of I-402. I'll tell you where it is."

"Chez Cafe. Sounds wonderful, like when your father and I honeymooned in Paris." Mom cupped her face in her hands. "We had the best food and even dinner on a yacht on the Seine. Did I tell you how I ordered snails and didn't even know it?"

Lindsey had heard this story a million times but she didn't mind because she always liked the way Mom's eyes lit up when she talked about those days. But today, Mom's eyes didn't sparkle or shine. Mom shook her head. "No, I'm not going to think about that. Those days are gone. Look for something cheaper."

"I'm looking for Elizabeth Taylor at the wax museum, and Dracula." Jenna raised her hand like Dracula when he was about to bite. "I vant to suck your blood, blahh, blah, blahh." She pushed the button to open the window separating them from the driver. "Drive on, Mr. Driver, sir! Drive on!" Then, she waved back to Dad who stood alone by his garage and abandoned inventions.

WHAT'S FOR BREAKFAST?

"I'll order first," Gwen said two hours later to the waitress. "I'll have fresh squeezed orange juice, croissant, preferably a pain au chocolat. But if all you have is a plain croissant, then include apricot jam."

Gwen placed her menu next to her stack of guidebooks. "I can be assured that your croissants are made with real butter, correct, so they are shaped like a tube? I'll also have eggs, scrambled, preferably farm raised. I'm famished from my packing and organizing." She patted her blonde streak. "I really had to take command or my family wouldn't be here. I've been up since 5:00 a.m. My vitality is zapped."

Lindsey startled up from her menu. People in cartoons might have $ signs popping out of their eyes, but exclamation points popped out of hers. How did Gwen know all those French foods?

"Honey, what kind of place do you think this is?" asked the waitress. Lindsey looked around at the torn seats and crooked tables. The waitress wore ordinary clothes, a bulky gray sweater and jeans, no uniform. They sat at a square table covered in a white plastic tablecloth, with salt and pepper shakers and stacks of sugar packets for a centerpiece. The chauffeur had said that he would eat a snack his wife had packed for him and wait for them in the limousine. Maybe he knew what he was doing. At least the waitress hadn't asked Lindsey if she wanted the children's menu.

"That's my Gwen." Mom patted Gwen's arm. "She always wants the best. You'll have to order what's on the menu, though, dear."

"I knew we should have stopped at Chez Café," Gwen said. "We're in Canada so we should eat French food. This menu is so, so, pedestrian." Gwen fanned the plastic menu with its bright pictures of pancakes, waffles, and eggs.

"This ain't no sidewalk, honey," the waitress replied. "Now what do you want to eat from the menu? In plain Canadian English."

"I'll have blueberry waffles," Gwen said. She looked deflated for once, but she flipped through her guidebook and started reading. "Did you know that there are several different falls? The Horseshoe Falls, the biggest one, drops 173 feet."

"I'm next, I'm next." Jenna bounced in her chair and smiled a round yellow smiley face smile. "Now, please, I'd very much like to have ..." and boom, her next bounce landed her on the floor. With only her eyes showing above the table, she said, "Eggs Benedict," and sat back up. Lindsey and Gwen laughed so hard they shook the table, wobbling the towers of jelly packets and sugars.

"Oops." Lindsey grabbed her water glass before she knocked it over.

"Now, girls. Enough. That was a good choice, Jenna," Mom said. "Something adventurous."

Jenna smiled like she'd won an Academy Award. Oh, no, it was Lindsey's turn. That switched off her laughter.

Lindsey folded the menu and then refolded. She studied it. A customer could order three eggs, two eggs, one egg, bacon, sausage, ham. Lindsey pushed her hair behind her and pulled it in front again, combing through and twisting it. She'd never be able to decide. Ah, that's it. She wouldn't decide. She'd let her finger do the work.

She shut her eyes, and punched her finger at her menu. For an instant she thrilled at the thought of what she'd chosen. She licked her lips, and opened her eyes. Oh, bother. Her finger pointed to eggs, sausage, and toast. How boring. She closed her eyes again and felt like crying.

"Oh, Lindsey, you only have to order breakfast, not decide your future." Mom breathed in deeply. Lindsey knew that sound—the sound of Mom's exasperation—she used it a lot with Lindsey. And, why did she have to talk about her future, when they knew the decision they had to make that weekend?

"She'll have an omelet," Mom said. Lindsey's eyes sprang open. An omelet! Mom knew she didn't like omelets.

"What kind of omelet?" The waitress asked, and shifted her weight to another hip.

"Cheese," Mom answered. "She'll have cheese. That will be good for you," she added, turning to Lindsey. "You can be so exasperating with your indecision, Lindsey." Then, Mom gently pressed her arm. Lindsey stuck her head behind her menu.

"I'll take that, dear," the waitress said. Lindsey released the menu and squeezed her eyes shut to catch any tears before they fell out.

When the omelet arrived, it resembled Jenna's smiley face smile, centered on an oval gray plate. Oh, why hadn't she made her own decision? She cut into the yellow gloppy eggy mess, and cheese seeped out the sides, like water running down the Falls. Lindsey gagged. She couldn't waste the food since it was their only meal out. They'd probably eat white bread sandwiches with American cheese for lunch—or worse. Worse? Could anything be worse?

Jenna and Gwen ate with more vigor. Jenna sawed at her Eggs Benedict and at the same time searched the restaurant for people to smile at, while Gwen ate with her pinkie finger in the air. *Crash*! Gwen's fork clattered to the floor.

"Oh, my goodness!" Mom stopped stirring her scrambled egg goo she hadn't been eating and dropped her fork as well.

Gwen picked up the forks and held them high. "I had my pinkie out, but you can't eat properly with forks manufactured for lumberjacks."

Mom sighed and reached in her purse for a pill bottle. She shook out a pill and swallowed it without drinking water. More sadness yanked at Lindsey's heart. Did Mom feel the cancer spreading in her body? Was that why they had to decide so fast, for Monday's treatment? But, no, she wouldn't think about it. If only the waitress hadn't taken her menu, she'd have something to read.

Mom smiled a weak smile. She folded her hands under her chin. "Now, girls, I want to talk to you seriously."

They were going to talk! Where was her book when she needed it?

Mom continued. "We're, I'm, all of us, are so disappointed in you, fighting twice before we left."

Gwen and Jenna had stopped eating and stared at Mom with their mouths open, a perfect description of dumbfounded, one of those words authors used in books but no one did in real life, except people who read too much, which might be her.

"I had hoped that you would step up to this challenge like your dad has. He has been so wonderful. He so wanted his business to take off, but things didn't work out and now he has to give it up for me and for you." She wept.

What did someone *do* when their mom was this sad?

Blowing her nose, Mom continued. "Since you girls continue to act out, we have no choice but to have you live with either Aunt Cassie or Aunt Angie. I know the aunts bicker, but I think they'll handle whatever decision you girls make."

Lindsey felt itchy. Everyone seemed to think that aunts' bickering was OK, but theirs wasn't. After all, they were kids and the aunts were grownups. It wasn't fair. She felt trapped. Could she say she had to go to the bathroom? After all, the waitress had filled her water glass so much that she could float to the Falls.

Lindsey stood up to leave. "Excuse me." A cold blast of air hit her in the back. Mom shivered and pulled her sweater tighter. A group of five high school boys rushed through the restaurant door. Boys! Cute boys like in *Tamera's Fortune*!

The boys tossed their hats back and forth to each other, and ran around the restaurant, pulling out chairs and sitting backward like cowboys. Some headed for the bathroom, slamming the door behind them. Four or five more poured through the restaurant door.

A boy wearing a thick blue sweater with a row of Xs switched in it took off his blue winter hat to reveal dark curly hair that swirled around his head in a perfectly wonderful swirly way. Definitely cute. If only he'd come closer, she could see the color of his eyes. If blue, he'd be perfection. Cuter than anyone Tamera dated in *How to Get a Date*.

The cute curly haired boy tossed his hat to another boy on the other side of the restaurant. "Throw the toque back to me, Marcus, eh?"

Torque? Lindsey thrilled to know what he would throw back.

The boy, who must be Marcus, tossed the hat to the curly haired boy on the other side. Oh, toque meant hat. Oh, she so wanted it to mean something more exotic. The other boy, Marcus, was shorter and built like a football player. His hair pointed upward while the other boy's curled under.

"Canadians talk different, eh?" Gwen laughed. "If only some of them spoke French. *Parlais vous Francais?*"

Mom covered her ears. "Those boys are so loud."

Jenna leapt up to look out the window and dashed back.

"It's a busload of boys. Do you think they're famous football players?" She sat down and laughed.

"It's Canada, dweeb," Gwen said. "They're probably hockey players. See if they have teeth."

A man as big as Hagrid, the giant in the Harry Potter books, pushed open the door. His beard stuck out straight from his chin like a stiff brush. He wore a blue windbreaker with the words Chinowapi High School Choir written in yellow. He yelled, "Boys, quiet! Sit down. NOW!"

The boys screeched their chairs across the floor and settled down immediately like kindergarteners at naptime.

Gwen leaned into Lindsey's ear, "Look at that hottie over there. The one with the blue sweater and the curly hair."

"I hadn't noticed him." Lindsey felt her face burn and eyeballed her omelet now cold and gluey. Double yuck.

"Which one, which one?" Jenna leaned in to hear.

"You're 11." Gwen pushed Jenna away. "Go back to your Barbies."

A hat whacked Lindsey on the head and flopped on the table in front of her. A silvery blue wool hat with thin red stripes—a toque. She touched it. It was as soft as a baby's. Oh, please let it be the curly haired hottie's hat.

"Hey, look, man. I got a girl." The boy with the curly hair laughed at pointy-haired Marcus. Oh, it *was*! It *was* his hat.

"Good one, Chris," Marcus yelled back. Oh, the hottie's name was Chris. In *High School Hottie*, Tamera's last date was with a boy named Chris.

Gwen slapped her hand down on the hat.

"Don't throw it back," she ordered. "Keep it. You always keep the stuff of the boy you have a crush on."

"I don't have a crush on him. Besides, where did you hear that?" Lindsey tucked her hair behind her ear.

"I'm 16 and I've been in high school a lot longer than you, and I know things. Trust me."

"Oh, I don't know. Shouldn't I throw it back?" She loosened her hair from behind her ear so it was free to be twisted—so much better for thinking.

"No." Gwen grabbed Lindsey's arm.

What should she do? Why could she never decide?

WE'RE HERE

Lindsey sat in a fog. She'd read *Tamera's Date* for the past several hours. She only had two more chapters to go, and she wanted to savor every word.

"Lindsey, are you coming?" Gwen called.

"Hmmm." Lindsey wrapped a strand of hair around her finger. Oh, to be Tamera.

"Lindsey!" Gwen stuck her head into the car window. "Are you an idiot?"

Lindsey jumped. "What? Oh, we've stopped." Only Mom sat in the limousine. "We're here?"

"Yes, we're here, Lindsey." Mom tapped her finger on Lindsey. "Stop reading. Now."

The chauffeur extended his hand into the back seat. "May I help you out of the car?" How romantic. He must think she's Tamera. Lindsey held out her hand to him, but he took Mom's instead. Oh, but how embarrassing. She rubbed her hands together pretending she'd reached out her hands, she could do just that, rub them. Of course, he'd help Mom, how stupid she was. Not Tamera at all.

Lindsey scrambled out the other side and rushed around to the back before the chauffeur could say anything but a gust of wind pushed her back toward her embarrassment. She fought against it and wrapped her gray coat tighter. Brrr. They'd parked behind a tall yellow brick building—maybe six floors high—whose sign read *Hotel Grandeur*. The building smashed against other yellow brick buildings running up a hill.

Lindsey sniffed the air. It didn't smell any different than home. She lifted her face. She didn't feel a mist. The only sound was the buzz of cars on the street. Wikipedia had said the sound of the Falls could drown out 20 supersonic jets and yet she heard nothing. How many miles away did that mean they were? It seemed strange that this hotel would be Aunt Angie and Uncle Marv's timeshare. Aunt Angie couldn't act all stuck up over this.

Gwen stood by the trunk with Jenna, who held onto her hat with both hands. The trunk performed its magic and opened displaying her suitcase lined up with the others.

"I'll help you with those," the chauffeur offered appearing next to Lindsey. He reached toward her suitcase.

Lindsey studied her suitcase, not acknowledging him. She wasn't going to say anything or look anywhere until she was sure he was talking to her.

"That's OK," Gwen replied for them all. "We can do it." Gwen lifted her brown suitcase and dropped it on the cracked gray pavement, *thwack*. From that sound Lindsey guessed that a library book or two might be hidden in Gwen's suitcase too.

"I'll be back for you at two o'clock on Sunday, Mrs. Rydell, unless you need my services." The chauffeur bent forward as he spoke and touched his hat.

"That'll be fine." Mom held her hand out for him to shake. "Thank you so much for getting us here safely." The chauffeur smiled and walked the long walk back to the front of the limousine.

Gwen smacked the curly haired boy's hat on Lindsey head. "Don't forget your theft. It's one sloppy hat. You could hide a rat in it. Meet you in the hotel, boy lover." Gwen headed to the hotel with Mom.

"Very funny." Lindsey pulled her suitcase out of the trunk. *Kerplunk.* Her clothes spilled out, and her books thumped across the parking lot.

The wind teased at the pink sweater, making the sleeves move as if the wind wanted it to run after Gwen and tattle. The next moment, the chauffeur waved his hand out the window, the trunk closed, and the limousine sped away.

"I'll help." Jenna tottered back to Lindsey on her heels, picking up a few blouses and the pink sweater on her way, wiping gravel from it. "You brought Gwen's pink sweater? She'll be hopping mad."

"You mean OPPSOOES." Lindsey laughed. "For One Pretty Pink Sweater Owned By One Evil Sister."

"Pink sweater is easier to say." Jenna tossed the sweater into the suitcase with the rest of the clothes. "How are you going to close it?"

Lindsey looked in despair at the mound of clothes rising from suitcase, "Oh, I don't know, I could ..." and then Jenna smashed it together and stuffed it under Lindsey's arm. Even Jenna knew how to take charge.

"Let's go." Jenna picked up her round white suitcase and white poodle and wobbled across the parking lot, her stick legs barely holding her up. She stopped and breathed deeply. "These heels are harder to walk in than they look." Jenna took her heels off and squished her feet into the pavement. "It's cold but, boy, do my feet hurt. I'll never believe a monster movie again. You know, the ones where the lady runs away from a monster in six-inch high heels. No one could do that in these. What shoes did you wear?" Jenna looked over. "Socks and flip flops? Why? Why would you be so impractical?"

"I was in a hurry and grabbed what I saw." Oh, bother. It did look weird—her big toe sticking out of the flip flop, all wrapped in white, an iceberg.

ADVENTURES IN GRANDEUR

Minutes later, Lindsey and Jenna pushed open the door to the front lobby.

"Oh, Hotel Grandeur is not only grand, it's beautiful!" Jenna twirled around the lobby. "Look at the chandelier, Lindsey. I'm getting dizzy."

"Chandelier? Where?" Lindsey searched the room.

"Up there!" Jenna pointed to a rectangular lamp hanging from the ceiling with dead bug juice clinging to its cord. Lindsey followed the cord down to a blue flowered carpet, with green stains like those on Aunt Cassie's clothes and slices in the carpet as if someone had used a razor blade.

Gwen poked her finger into a rip in the arm of a chair that had flowered upholstery and clawed feet. "This rips big enough to lose your arm in. Aunt Angie sure overstated facts about Uncle Marv's timeshare. When I move to Paris, I'm staying only at the very best hotels along the River Seine. And, I'm living there forever—not just honeymooning."

Lindsey touched the wad of money in her pocket. She could tell Mom that they could afford to stay somewhere nicer. But that wouldn't work. She'd give her the look she only gave Lindsey, the one Lindsey got at breakfast, and then follow with a lecture on the importance of honesty. Finally, she'd have to personally give the money back to Aunt Angie, saying how sorry she was for taking it. Money that was offered to them, but Mom wouldn't remember that. No, Lindsey would have to spend it without Mom knowing. She pushed the money deeper into her pocket.

"Do you think those boys followed us here?" Jenna asked. "We could find out what room they're in and call them." Jenna held her pinkie and thumb to her face as if talking on a cell phone. "Hello, this is Jenna. Oh, yes, I am beautiful, aren't I?" Jenna strutted around the room. "Call me sometime."

Lindsey felt her face flame, knowing she wasn't brave enough or slightly crazy enough to call. If she called the curly haired boy, she'd stammer and stutter and say, "Um, Hi," and then freeze. Besides, you couldn't call up and say, "It's me. The girl who stole your hat."

Lindsey's heart thumped at the thought. If she did call him, it would be the first time she ever called a boy. Last year, she almost called Evan from her Algebra class for homework help but hung up because everyone knew she didn't need help.

"Well, if they followed anyone, it was me." Gwen flipped her hair to show off her natural blonde streak.

At the thought of an entire bus turning around for Gwen, Lindsey laughed. She imagined the Hagrid-like man yelling to the bus driver, "Follow that limo!" And the bus screeching it tires and turning around on the narrow highways that had brought them here, all the while the boys' eyes stared bugged eye out the window at Gwen. No, that didn't happen. The boys aren't here, and they certainly didn't turn around and follow them.

At the front desk, the clerk handed Mom a key card. "Thank you, I'm sure we're going to enjoy our stay." She backed away from the front desk toward Lindsey and her sisters.

Gwen said into Lindsey's ear. "I think the clerk is watching me. I'm sure he's in college." Lindsey looked at the clerk: a skinny scarecrow with dandruff on his shoulders and grease on his tie.

"You can have him, Gwen." Lindsey brushed the air. "I guess I don't like college boys. Right, Jenna?"

"Right, we're looking for *good looking* boys. Perhaps you don't know the meaning." Jenna focused straight into Gwen's eyes and blinked. "Maybe you can try one of your personalities on him."

"Let's find our room," Mom said. "It's 324."

Gwen took Mom's suitcase and headed for the elevator.

"I'll beat you there." Jenna sped toward the heavy metal door to the stairs and opened it. She teetered on her heels, but started up. "Come on, Lindsey, follow me."

"You'll sweat, Jenna," Gwen yelled after her. "French people don't sweat." The elevator opened and Gwen and Mom stepped in.

Lindsey froze. Should she get in or follow Jenna? Before she could decide, the elevator closed and Gwen and Mom disappeared. Another decision made for her. Now she had to follow Jenna. Why was Jenna always so impulsive?

She entered the stairwell and yelled, "Jenna, wait up," but Jenna was out of sight, only her high heels clattered overhead like angels tap dancing out of sight. Her antelope figure made her quick. Lindsey heard a door slam and the sound of Jenna's heels faded. As they did, the emergency light on her landing blinked off leaving her alone in a dark stairwell that smelt damp and metallic and scary. Had she wanted to be scared like this, she could have stayed home.

She moved forward, but fell on a step and tumbled onto the landing. Ow! She'd stubbed her unprotected big toe. She moved to stand but heard breathing and stopped. Close breathing. Close enough for the person to be staring deep into her pimples. She squeezed her eyes shut and waited for the person to grab her. But nothing. Just more harsh breathing. She had to know what or who it was. She'd wanted to die with her eyes open, to die brave.

She opened her eyes and glanced around into the dark corners of the landing. In the corner of the landing, a vent blasted hot air every few seconds. Oh, how stupid. Nothing but a vent. She needed Jenna to get her out of here and onto the right floor.

"Jenna?" Her voice echoed back. "Jenna!" Oh, but Jenna couldn't hear her anymore. She was in Room *XXX*, nice and safe with Mom. Lindsey could go back down to the elevator, but an empty elevator that stopped at every floor and let in strangers would be just as bad as continuing up these stairs.

Lindsey resumed her trudge up the stairs. At each step, the metal stairs rang out their emptiness. Her arm cramped. Oh, if she could only let go of this suitcase. And, she couldn't lift her legs because of her too-tight jeans. And her flip flops wouldn't flop. Shaking from exhaustion, she stopped at the third landing and leaned against the wall to catch her breath, her hair sticking into the cement block walls.

"The third floor. Do room numbers match the floor?" she asked the stairs. "What was the room number? Hmmm … It was something in order, like 432 or 543." She felt the darkness closing in. A man may not be breathing on her like she thought, but a metallic ghost might be: one that cracked his metallic knuckles. "Lindsey," she encouraged herself. "You've got to keep moving."

She climbed one more flight of stairs to the fourth. She heard a faint click and a door slammed overhead. Someone had entered the stairs for real.

"I'm getting out of here!" She opened the door to the fourth floor. She couldn't believe what she saw. Boys! It positively rained high school boys! A riot of boys filled the long corridor.

"Oh," she gasped, as she saw the curly haired boy, Chris, from the restaurant drinking from the water fountain. She remembered his name better than she remembered the room number. Behind him stood Marcus. So cute. They were definitely better looking than the boys Tamera had dated in *Tamera Turns Seventeen*. What a good book that had been. Tamera had worn a yellow dress to her Junior prom. Junior proms. They didn't have those at her school.

Chris spun around. "Hey, there's the girl with my hat."

Lindsey jumped back from the world of yellow prom dresses to the hallway of a rundown hotel. She touched her head. The hat still covered her head. She'd forgotten it.

"Yeah, it's her, all right," Marcus said. "She's wearing the evidence. Hey, chick!" Marcus raised his hand toward her.

Lindsey looked around to see if he could be talking to someone else. But no such luck this time. She pointed to herself.

"Yeah, you."

At that moment, a large man in blue stepped in front of Lindsey. It was the Hagrid look-alike from the restaurant.

"What are you doing on this floor, young lady?" he boomed.

"Oh, um."

"The young ladies are on the fifth floor. I'll escort you to the elevator and back to the fifth." He pointed in the direction of the elevator.

"Well, actually, I can go back down the stairs here. I must've gotten off at the wrong floor."

He scowled like he didn't believe her. "No, miss, I will take you to the elevator and press the button to ensure that you go to the fifth floor. Follow me."

Lindsey marched behind him. She could feel the curly haired boy staring at her. She touched her head to be sure the hat was still there. When she did, her suitcase fell open. She watched all her stuff—like her life—flash before her eyes. Her romance and dog books lay exposed, even the picture book about Annie.

"Oh, no!"

Mr. Hagrid man whipped around and his eyes burned into her. Marcus laughed.

"My suitcase. It, it has a bad lock." She knelt to scoop up a book and her clothes, including OPPSOOES. Oh, please, she prayed, let my underwear still be in my suitcase. Whew. It was. A book appeared in the corner of her eye. Someone was handing her the book *High School Loves*. She slowly glanced upward to see Chris handing it to her with a slight crooked smile.

"Thank you." She prayed again that he hadn't noticed the title.

"Chris and Marcus, leave the lady in peace," Mr. Hagrid man said.

"But she's got—"

"Never mind, boys. Leave."

Chris and Marcus walked away mumbling something about freezing in Niagara Falls in November (what stupid school makes you go to Niagara Falls in November anyway?) and how they didn't like frozen, red ears when they sang in front of a crowd.

They're probably best friends, Lindsey thought, watching them retreat. In *How to Get a Date*, Tamera dated two best friends at the same time. Maybe she could do that, too. Maybe Chris and Marcus were 17 and drove and they'd drive to her house and bring her flowers and take her for a ride in their red convertible, and Mom would wave to them because she would be well—

"If you are quite done, young lady," Mr. Hagrid man said interrupting her. "We can continue to the elevator and send you to the fifth floor where you belong." Lindsey nodded. She noticed his name badge, Walter Kleptomanie.

When the elevator door opened, Lindsey entered. Walter pressed the elevator button and sent her zooming to the fifth floor.

MOVING ON UP

Number 5 lit up on the elevator panel and the door opened. Lindsey snuck out, not sure what was ahead. Yikes! As many high school girls ran around the fifth floor as boys had on the fourth.

"What are you doing?" asked a woman who looked like she belonged in the army, her hair in a severe bun, her shoulders back, and her rather large bosom pointing forward. She carried a clipboard. Lindsey and the lady met eye to eye. "Why are you late?"

"I'm not late," Lindsey answered. "I just got here."

"Doctor Schwab says you are late. What room are you in?"

"I don't remember. That's my problem." Lindsey replied and then wondered who Doctor Schwab was and how he knew she was late. Maybe this was some kind of clinic. Girls screeched past her and ran down the hall in pink and purple sweats, running into rooms and shutting doors. One girl with long blonde hair wore shorts and long green socks with pink and red flowers sewn on. Cute. Maybe she could get a pair like that with Aunt Angie's money. After all, she had lots of it, but she knew her conscience would flatten her if she spent it on that.

"I have it here on my clipboard. 524. You should have asked Dr. Schwab." The lady checked off something on her clipboard. "You're the girl arriving with her parents. Come with me."

Lindsey followed behind. As they passed a room in the hall, the girls screeched and ran inside slamming the doors shut.

To each slamming door, the lady called, "Yes, Doctor Schwab is ready to check on you too. No monkey business."

When the last door slammed shut, quiet engulfed the hall. Lindsey felt itchy and uncomfortable. Who was this Doctor Schwab and what he would do when he got there? Being with this lady might be safer than running into Doctor Schwab.

Lindsey matched her step to the woman and squared her shoulders. She might as well be in the army. Go here, go there, do this, do that. Maybe she'd like it, no decisions to make. Her hair might look better pinned back anyway. Aunt Angie always said it was too stringy. Of course, then she couldn't twist it to think, and where would she be?

She sighed and considered the woman in front of her marching down the quiet hall. She really shouldn't follow a stranger even if Doctor Schwab lurked somewhere. She needed to find Mom. Something could have happened to her and she'd need the money. She should speak up and stop this, but she still didn't know their room number. If Gwen were here, she'd think of a plan. Gwen! That's it. She'd ask the scarecrow clerk at the front desk. If he had a crush on Gwen, he'd have memorized the room number.

She'd done it. A decision, a plan! Unless … Unless, because of rules, he couldn't tell her. But no, she'd act like Gwen and flirt with him. Right, sure. She slumped back to her normal posture. She didn't know how to flirt. Well, she'd worry about that when she got there. She'd interrupt the woman now.

Lindsey throat suddenly felt thick with fear. She cleared it. "Ahem."

The woman kept marching, her shoulders straight on toward the inevitable 524. Lindsey pursed her lips. She had to get her attention.

"Excuse me," Lindsey said louder. "I'd like to, I mean, where is, I should be …"

The woman stopped. Great! Even with her jumbled speech, the woman was going to listen. See, it wasn't so difficult to take charge.

Instead of listening, the woman knocked three sharp knocks on the door. Lindsey read the room number, 524. The woman had only stopped to knock at room 524. Well, that helped. Room numbers *do* match floor numbers. Now if she could only remember the room number, she'd be set.

After no answer, the woman talked into the door, her lips almost touching the metal. "Miss Burke, your roommate has arrived." The woman spun around to stare at Lindsey. "Late."

No answer still. The woman put her eye to the peephole.

"Miss Burke. Open at once." She knocked several more times.

The doorknob twisted and a girl Gwen's age cracked the door, her dark hair pulled back in a ponytail with no makeup or jewelry.

"Hello, Doctor Schwab," the girl said.

"Yes, Doctor Schwab is here," the lady said. "I have your roommate." She tapped on her clipboard.

Oh! *Doctor Schwab* was the woman she'd been following! The lady talked about herself in the third person! Gwen would call her an idiot for not being aware of a stranger danger alert.

"My roommate, great." Miss Burke pulled Lindsey into her room, only opening it wide enough for Lindsey to squeeze through, which knocked open Lindsey's suitcase. Again! Miss Burke pushed the door shut on Doctor Schwab. "Thank you, Doctor Schwab. Good bye."

Doctor Schwab shoved back on the door and entered, "Thank you for inviting Doctor Schwab in." Doctor Schwab scanned the room as if searching for something, but it would be hard to find anything in that room. Clothes crawled out of an open suitcase in search of freedom like Lindsey's kept doing. A Jim Thorton's coffee cup tipped on the floor almost spilling its contents. Total chaos.

Doctor Schwab picked up a red thick wool sweater on the bed and then laid it back down. "Well, Miss Meredith Burke meet Miss Lisa, your roommate."

"Hi, Lisa." Meredith nodded

Lindsey waved a small wave. "Hi."

Doctor Schwab paced the room. She lifted a shampoo bottle from the dresser and sniffed it. She moved to the closet and opened it. Nothing but hangers and an iron. What was Doctor Schwab looking for?

Meredith opened the door. "I'm sure we're going to get along great. You can leave now, Doctor Schwab. Thanks."

Lindsey almost hoped that Doctor Schwab wouldn't leave. What was this girl doing that made Doctor Schwab so suspicious?

"Doctor Schwab is always walking the halls, girls," Doctor Schwab said as she left. "Always on patrol."

"Good bye, Doctor." Meredith closed the door behind her. She faced Lindsey, and stared with her open freckled face and ponytail. Lindsey felt a wave of sympathy for this girl—her roommate—but then fear overtook the sympathy when Meredith said:

"You're not going to tell on me, are you?" she bit a fingernail.

"No, of course not." Lindsey twirled her hair and pushed it behind her ear, and pulled it out for more twisting—serious situations required serious hair twisting. "Why would I tell on you?"

Meredith rushed to her bed and searched through the bed sheets. Lindsey moved closer to the door and her suitcase as she watched Meredith. What was she getting? Drugs? Gwen had told her about older kids and drugs. Lindsey thought that she better get out of here but she hesitated. What should she do? Then Lindsey noticed Meredith's lumberjack clothes, plaid shirt, jeans, and boots. Perhaps Meredith was searching for her gun. Something to threaten her with so she wouldn't tell.

Meredith stopped thrashing and dragged something out from under the covers: a lump the size of a, a bomb! Maybe Lindsey was in a new book of the Tamera series, *Tamera Meets the Terrorist*. She placed her hand on her heart ready for her fate. She was a goner.

Yip!

Meredith had pulled out a brown and white dog, all hair, and pink bow and red tongue. The sweetest, darlingest dog Lindsey had ever seen, and the very kind that she and Jenna wanted—a dog to the stars.

"Oh, that is, like, so cute." Lindsey ran to pet it, forgetting to be afraid of Meredith. The dog licked Lindsey with its little sandpaper tongue. It tickled. Lindsey tilted her head back and laughed. "Oh, I love your dog." Lindsey couldn't stop petting it. It was like petting Mom's satin wedding dress.

"She likes you, too." Meredith patted the bed beside her for Lindsey to sit. "She's Ginger, named after the movie star in *Gilligan's Island*, my dad's favorite show when he was a kid."

"What kind of a dog is she?" Lindsey asked, thinking it looked like a Yorkshire Terrier but it was too tiny to be one.

"She's a teacup," Meredith said.

Lindsey cocked her head. The dog was a teacup? "A what?" Lindsey asked.

"A teacup. Ginger's an extra small dog—and extra expensive. A teacup-sized Yorkshire Terrier."

Oh, it was a *kind* of Yorkshire Terrier.

"You were allowed to bring her on your class trip?"

"No, of course not. That's why I hid her and drove Doctor Schwab out of here ASAP. She'd have put me in what my grandma used to call a *kerfuffle*." Meredith patted Ginger's head pushing her ears back.

A *kerfuffle*? A torque, a teacup, and now a kerfuffle. And Canadians said they spoke English.

"Don't tell." Meredith bit another nail. "Ginger is well ... she's ... anyway, I told my mom we could bring small dogs. That's one good thing about a mom who doesn't pay attention." Meredith studied Lindsey while she started on another fingernail. "How come I've never seen you at school?"

"Oh, I don't go to your school." Lindsey slid her toe over to the spilt Jim Thorton's cup and pushed against it. A trickle of coffee escaped. Lindsey jerked her foot back.

"Then how can you be on this trip? Are you a famous singer or something? We're expecting a soloist to join us. You're not her?"

Lindsey gasped. "Ah, no. I got lost looking for my mom and sisters. Doctor Schwab only thought I was your roommate."

"Really? Too bad, you'd have been a good roommate. You look like someone a person can trust."

Lindsey's heart skipped a victory lap in her chest. Wow, that made her feel good, the best she'd felt in days. Maybe she could stay here with Meredith. She could dress like a lumberjack and throw away OPPSOOES. Mom and her aunts would think she'd run away or died. Oh, no, not *died*. How could she even think that word?

59

Her thoughts were interrupted when Meredith said, "Hey, wait a minute. If you're not my roommate, then Doctor Schwab will be coming back with my real one. That isn't good. You'd better get out of here. Take Ginger."

"What?"

"Take my dog. *Please?* Keep her for me until tomorrow. It's your fault that Schwab is coming back here. She's gonna be suspicious."

"My fault? Take your dog?" Lindsey's head hurt. She needed to get out of this nightmare.

"Sure, put Ginger in that funny hat you're wearing. As soon as Schwab leaves, I'll come down. I'll text you. What's your number?"

"I don't have a cell phone."

"You don't? Really? I never heard of someone without a phone. Are you crazy, like in a religious cult? Or a vegetarian?"

"No, but—" Lindsey twisted her hair around and around. Oh, what a strange karma day.

Meredith stopped arguing and crammed Lindsey's clothes into her suitcase. She pushed down to shut it. "Hey, this won't shut."

"Smash it together and put it under my arm." What was she saying? She was helping the girl perpetrate fraud! Like in, like in, well, like in real life!

Meredith tucked the suitcase under Lindsey's right arm. Then, she ripped Lindsey's hat off her head and fitted Ginger into it, stretching the hat tight over Ginger's legs and head, letting only her nose show. What an amazing dog to let someone do that. So cute! Oh, Lindsey's heart warmed to that little plump dog.

"Gin-gin, Mommy loves you. You're going to stay with Lisa." Meredith kissed the dog's nose and patted her head. "Here take her. What room are you in?"

"Oh, um, it's something in order." Lindsey hugged the dog against her with her free hand. "Hmmm ..." She badly wanted to twist her hair to help her think but her load of dog and suitcase stopped her. Then it came to her. "It's 324."

"Great, I'll be there to get her before we leave. You know, maybe I should tell you one thing about her." Meredith looked at Lindsey a long time like she was focusing a camera. Then, she said, "Never mind, it won't matter. Get going."

"But—"

Meredith opened the door. "Better get out of here before Doctor Schwab sees you."

WHAT A MESS!

"Boo!" Jenna opened the door of their hotel room to let Lindsey in. Gwen stood behind her, glaring.

Lindsey dropped her suitcase and its contents splattered over the floor, her only guaranteed karma. She stepped over the clothes and looked around. The room seeped beige—beige curtains, beige carpeting, beige furniture—as if it had surrendered all its color. Two double beds bumped up against one wall and a T.V. and desk bumped up against the other. Squished in one corner was a small kitchen with a mini refrigerator and scrunched in another corner was a tiny beige couch next to a fireplace. If they still played house, it would be perfect.

Mom slept on the farthest bed, her hand tangled in her hair. Lindsey wished she could smooth it out. It looked so messed and confused. It must be horrible to be sick and not know if you're going to get well. She shook her head to push away those thoughts and get back to the dogs and boys.

"Where have you been?" Gwen asked in a loud whisper. "You should be grounded. You didn't even help unpack, except for dumping your clothes all over the floor, thank you very much."

"Oh, it keeps happening, no stopping karma. Anyway, you'll never believe what I found." Lindsey scanned back and forth from Jenna to Gwen hoping for an audience for her terrific news.

Gwen yawned. "What do I care what you found?" She lay down on the empty bed and examined her fingernails. The beige bedspread made of whatever unknown plastic sprang up around her instead of wrinkling.

"I found the boys." Lindsey beamed like a mouse with a cookie.

"The boys!" Jenna shrieked and jumped on the bed, bouncing around Gwen. "Let's call them. Let's call the boys."

"Shh, you'll wake up Mom," Gwen said, this time in a real whisper. She yanked Jenna down to a sitting position. Jenna wiggled free and stepped in front of Lindsey.

"The boys," Jenna said in a low gravelly voice and stuck her tongue out at Gwen.

"Yes," Lindsey answered in a fake whisper like she was Dracula answering Frankenstein. She stuck out her tongue at Gwen, as well. "The boys from the restaurant. They saw me with this hat." Lindsey held the hat aloft, now fat and lumpy and overflowing with its dog contents. "They're on the fourth floor."

"The fourth floor? What were you doing on the fourth floor, Lindsey? Kissing one of them?" Jenna kissed her hand again and again. "Oh, boy, whose hat I stole, I love you!"

Lindsey yanked Jenna's hand down. "Stop it, Jenna, I was not. I climbed to the wrong floor. I knew I should've thrown the hat back."

"Why didn't you?" Gwen asked.

"I don't know. I wasn't sure what to do." Lindsey shrugged. Then she smiled. "I also found something else." Lindsey held the hat even higher. "Something wonderful. You'll never believe it."

"What, what, what?" Jenna jumped up and down. "Is it in the hat? Is that why it's all lumpy? Is it something for me?"

"No, it's not for you. I found a girl."

"There's a girl in that hat?" Jenna asked.

"Very funny. No, I found a girl who asked me to take care of her dog." Lindsey cuddled the hat close to her and pulled it down to reveal a bright red bow attached to a dog.

"A dog! A dog! There's a dog in there? Is it an Elizabeth Taylor dog?" Jenna grabbed for the hat.

At that, Mom moaned and sat up. "What? Has something happened? You're not fighting?"

"It's OK, Mom." Gwen patted Mom's arm and put the covers over her shoulders. "Go back to sleep. We were organizing our stuff." Gwen motioned for them to talk in the bathroom. She opened the door and she and Lindsey squeezed in.

Jenna shoved against the door. "Guys, aren't you going to let me in? Gee."

"There's no room. Hold on," Gwen said. "Lindsey, step behind the door so Jenna can come in."

"Gosh, you guys are mean." Jenna pressed her way in. "Not letting me in."

"No, we *couldn't* let you in because bathroom is too small and beige!" Lindsey said. The bathroom was only as wide as a hallway with a bath, sink, and toilet. Gwen shut the door and Lindsey elbowed her way around Jenna to the beige round sink. She laid the hat in it, and Ginger scrambled out like a celebrity appearing from behind a curtain.

"Oh, I want it. I want it," Jenna said. "It *is* an Elizabeth Taylor dog! It's what I was praying for." She picked up Ginger and Ginger yipped and yipped. Startled like she'd seen a celebrity in real life, Jenna dropped her. "She's not very friendly."

"It's a lumpy looking dog." Gwen poked Ginger's stomach.

"Yeah, a little," Jenna agreed. Lindsey agreed too but she wasn't going to say so.

"It's just fat from being held all the time," Jenna said. "If I had a dog like that, I'd never put it down—not even to sleep." This time Jenna held her fingers to Ginger's nose. Ginger sniffed and licked them. "She probably likes Eggs Benedict."

"You offered to take care of it?" Gwen petted Ginger and glanced in the mirror. She straightened her hair with her other hand, inspecting her blonde streak. Gwen's way of multitasking. What did she think anyway, that one day her streak would disappear?

"No, not really," Lindsey answered. "The girl told me to care of it until they leave so she won't get in trouble with Doctor Schwab."

"But we're *not* just taking care of it." Jenna attempted to pick her up again. This time it worked and Ginger snuggled in her arms. "We're *keeping* her. Boy is her tummy strange."

"You're both crazy," Gwen said and Ginger yipped.

Lindsey took Ginger from Jenna, and rubbed her cheek in Ginger's long hair. The little dog snuggled in her arms. Lindsey's heart softened and felt as mushy as when she read the book about the teenager who had to be in a wheelchair for the rest of her life and yet her boyfriend still loved her. Lindsey knew she wanted the dog as much as Jenna did.

"I should have figured you didn't offer to take it," Gwen said. "But this one is up to you. It's not my problem. I've got enough taking care of Mom since you do nothing."

"Who said I needed or wanted your help?" Lindsey sat down on the edge of the tub with the dog. Jenna scooted next to her, petting Ginger.

"We can do anything we want," Jenna said. "Right, Lindsey? We're very responsible and sufficient."

"Yes, we are," Lindsey said, but she sure didn't like being responsible for this dog. How did she know what to do?

"Right, you two don't need my help," Gwen said. "That's a laugh. Have you even thought about where you'll live?"

"It's a tough decision for me because—" Jenna tossed her hair, "*everyone* loves me. The cuckoo aunts are practically on their knees begging me." Jenna smiled her smiley face smile. "But *I* love them too. Seriously, Aunt Cassie is, like, so yummy and warm, and Aunt Angie is so rich and would give me a dog, but I've got one." Jenna rubbed Ginger's ears as if she were giving them a scrub. She said in a squeaky voice, "Gin-gin, my love."

"You don't even know that dog." Gwen poked Ginger's stomach again. "It probably has a tumor."

"You know, Linds, we should stick together." Jenna rubbed her head into Lindsey's arm like a cat. "Live with the same aunt and maybe the same dog."

"Well, right, of course, but, maybe, I don't know." Lindsey twisted a strand of her hair.

Jenna pouted her bottom lip. "You're not very sure. I'm loyal even if you're not."

"I put together a list." Gwen pulled a sheet of paper from her jeans. "Of pros and cons. Living with Aunt Cassie: con, she'll make us cook her crazy food and clean her house. Living with Aunt Angie: con, too far from school, but of course, she might let us take a limousine to school. Con: she's bossy. Con: she's sometimes mean. Only problem is the person I want to live with has more cons. So, what do you think, Linds?"

"I don't know. I mean, you know how forgetful Dad is. Maybe if we don't say anything, he'll forget about making us leave. Maybe Mom isn't so sick."

"Lindsey, that is so illogical; it's almost pathetic," Gwen said. "You have to decide."

Before Lindsey could move, Gwen gave her a quick hug, enough to be called a hug but not too touchy. Just like Gwen. Gwen was probably right too. Not making a decision hadn't been working—no window seat, an omelet for breakfast, stairs not elevator. But still, what if she did choose, and Mom didn't get well, and they never went home, and the person she choose became her family? No, she wouldn't think about it and she wouldn't decide.

"Will we still be sisters if we go different places?" Jenna asked. "I don't want different sisters."

Lindsey said, "Oh, Jenna," and she laughed and was surprised when Gwen joined her. Encouraged by Gwen's laughter, she gave Jenna a shove. Jenna jumped up and shoved her back.

"Whoa, I'm falling." Lindsey fell into the tub. Her shoulder bumped the faucet and scalding water sprayed her and Ginger, creating their own Niagara Falls. "Help me! Gwen!"

"Ginger is drowning!" Jenna jumped up and down. "She's going to die."

"Oh, stop yelling." Gwen shut off the shower and jerked Lindsey to a sitting position on the tub's edge. Lindsey inspected Ginger. She no longer rated a 10, with her lovely bow askew and her fur in a tangle.

"Your dog's a drowned rat." Gwen placed her hand on her hip.

"Don't call Gin-Gin a rat," yelled Jenna. "You're an old poo head boss."

"Oh, stop acting like a baby," Gwen yelled back. "You've been acting like you're seven this whole trip."

"Girls, girls, what are you doing in there?" It was Mom. "Are you fighting again? You can't even make an effort for our last weekend together?"

"Will you two *do* something!" Gwen ordered motioning to the water from the shower that had formed puddles in the grime between the beige tiles and in the corners. "Mom's going to come in."

Lindsey pulled a long strand of toilet paper and wiped Ginger. The toilet paper disintegrated into a pile of fuzz. Jenna handed her a bunch of tissues.

"For Pete's sake!" Gwen snatched the tissues. "I can't stand it when you're idiots." She pulled down a pile of towels and placed Ginger on them. She offered the pile to Lindsey. "Take care of your fat rat. I'll dry the floor. But from now on, it's up to you. I'm not helping anymore. You can't be this hopeless."

Gwen opened the door to Mom. Her curly hair stood out like a rooster's peak.

"My goodness, you took a long time." She rushed past them, not noticing the pile of towels Lindsey carried with Ginger on top. "Lindsey, do something with that suitcase, please."

Lindsey headed to her suitcase, and plopped the towels on top of her clothes. She draped several of them over the upright suitcase cover to create a tent for Ginger. Why couldn't she think of things like this when Gwen was around?

"Are we stealing those towels?" Jenna asked. "There's more stuff we could steal. The tiny lotions in the bathroom are sweet. We could sell them on eBay."

"Where are the towels?" Mom called from the bathroom. "What have you done with all the towels?" Lindsey scrambled to the bathroom with one.

A few minutes later, Mom crawled back into bed. She fluffed her pillows and asked, "So, who's sleeping where? Have you girls decided?"

Oh, bother, Lindsey thought, here it goes again. If she decided wrong, Jenna would cry and Gwen would harass her.

Gwen flopped on the empty bed. "This is mine."

"And, this is mine." Jenna flopped on the other, and snuggled with Mom. She brushed the hair from Mom's cheek and kissed her. Lindsey felt a tug on her heart. Now, she wouldn't get to sleep with Mom. Indecision was like indigestion.

"That was settled easily. See, you girls *can* work together. Now we need something to eat. You girls run over to the Food Lion. Buy a loaf of bread, some apples, cheese, and some kind of lunch meat. We could have a picnic right here in front of the fire. Won't that be fun? We'll have a good talk. Later, we can walk down to the Falls and see them lit up at night. And tomorrow, the wax museum."

"Yeah! The wax museum!" Jenna jumped up and down on the bed.

Lindsey ignored them and rooted around in her suitcase for her next book. Which should she read? This would be a fun decision, one that only mattered to her. She'd read, turn a page, pet Ginger, read, turn a page, pet Ginger. Delicious.

Lindsey dug up *High School Loves*. The towel tent moved. She peeked under it. Ginger tugged at the pink sweater and arranged it around her for a bed.

"Ginger, that's Gwen's sweater—the OPPSOOES." Lindsey said in a whisper. "I'm wearing it to the museum tomorrow." Lindsey imagined Chris showing up at the museum and not even caring about his hat because Lindsey looked so ravishing in the pink sweater, as if she were sixteen, maybe even seventeen. If only she'd bought the eye shadow and a pink lipstick too. She'd be a real wow. Chris might ask her out for a Coke or even a coffee at Jim Thorton's. If Meredith could drink it, maybe she could—

"Lindsey, honey, what are you doing?" Lindsey looked up to see Mom standing over her. Startled, Lindsey dropped the towel over Ginger. Luckily, Ginger had squirreled into OPPSOOES.

"I'm choosing a book to read, only I can't decide. Aren't these great?" She held up *High School Loves* and *Celebrity Dogs*, leaving the picture book about Annie hidden. "I finished all the ones in the Tamera series."

"Honey, we're in Niagara Falls. It's not time to read. It's time to *live*." At the word *live*, Mom cried softly. Ginger peeked her nose, then her eyes, and finally her entire head from behind the towel and whimpered. Lindsey dumped another towel over her. She looked up to see Jenna wrapping her arms around Mom and Gwen handing her a tissue.

"Big squeeze," Jenna said. "Like Daddy gives."

Again, Lindsey hadn't helped Mom. Instead, she'd made it worse. Maybe Mom was right and she should be sent away. At the thought, her heart cracked and she felt like an orphan in an old movie.

Gwen gave Lindsey a "see what you did" look. Lindsey shrugged in despair. Gwen mouthed to Lindsey to say Sorry, but instead Mom said it.

"Sorry." She blew her nose. "I'm a little shaky right now. You girls go and get our picnic food, and I'll be much better when you get back. I think I need to visit the bathroom again. A towel please." She held out her hand. Lindsey's eyes fixed on the towels. What to do? Jenna quickly moved in front of the suitcase and Lindsey grabbed the top towel and handed it to Mom.

"My goodness," Mom said. "You'd think those towels were holding something precious."

While they put on their coats to go to the store, Gwen asked, "Now what are you going to do with the dog, Miss Smarty Pants?"

"I'll take Ginger with me in the hat, so there." Lindsey gathered Ginger from behind the towel tent. She felt damp. With her snarled hair and crooked bow, they better not see Meredith or she'd discover the true Lindsey: someone you did not want for a roommate, someone positively not to be trusted. She tucked Ginger in the hat and under the front of her coat.

"Does she have any food?" Gwen asked.

"Oh no, she doesn't." Lindsey slapped her forehead. "I didn't think of that. What should we do?"

"Don't look at me. I told you this is your problem, remember?"

Lindsey reached into the pocket of her coat. Her finger found a hole. Oh, no! The money from Aunt Angie was gone! She'd lost over $100. But wait. She switched the hand that held Ginger and dug into the other pocket. Whew, it was in the other one.

She waved the money in the air. "Babysitting money! I was going to buy souvenirs but now I'll buy dog food. I've got it all taken care of."

"That's not babysitting money," Jenna called. "You're lying. I saw Aunt Angie—" Lindsey dropped the money and clamped her free hand over Jenna's mouth.

Jenna pulled away from Lindsey and picked up the money. She riffled through it like a gambler. "You never babysat enough to earn this much money!"

"Give it to me, Jenna." Lindsey held out her hand.

"Stop arguing," Gwen said. "You'll bother Mom. Give her the money, Jenna. It's probably all $1's." Gwen opened the door. "Do you have a leash? That dog probably needs to go to the bathroom."

"I'll buy one at the store. I'll let her do her business in the park on our way back." Lindsey held up her free hand like a traffic cop and said, "Stop, before you say anything else. I've thought of everything. I'm so in control, I'm even going to organize my suitcase when we get back and make my decision." Lindsey only wished she was.

ROARING THROUGH THE LION

"Who's going to buy this for me?" Jenna held up a snow globe with Niagara Falls inside. She shook it and gold glitter floated onto the foaming white plastic water of the Falls. Bright lights glinted off it from overhead. They were in the front of the Food Lion superstore, two blocks from their hotel. On the way, they'd passed a Dollar Store; Pete's Souvenir's, Tattoos, and Ear Piercing; and three boarded-up houses.

Lindsey thought she'd seen enough beige in their condo, but the Food Lion's beige linoleum floor swirled like fudge ripple ice cream, and its beige display cases and colorless hanging lights created a dull, boring, drab Lion.

"Too tacky." Gwen took the snow globe from Jenna and placed it back on the glass display, next to rows and rows of other snow globes, some as big as footballs and others as tiny as thimbles, some with the Niagara Falls in them, others with snowman, penguins, and even geese, and what snowmen, penguins, and geese had to do with Niagara Falls, Lindsey didn't know. "Everything here is tacky," Gwen added.

"You could buy it for me, Lindsey." Jenna picked it back up and placed it in Lindsey's palm. "With all your gobs and gobs of precious mullah."

Lindsey hesitated before she answered. She studied the other Niagara Falls souvenirs: lava lamps with a picture of Niagara Falls etched on them while inside red globs bobbed up and down; purple plush toys shaped like the Falls; even gum with the Falls logo. All these pictures of Niagara Falls and she hadn't even seen them for real yet.

After surveying the souvenirs, Lindsey shrugged. "I don't know, maybe I could buy it for you." She fingered the money in her pocket. Aunt Angie would want Jenna to have her heart's desire, but Jenna's heart desired everything, and besides, what if there was a horrible accident and they needed to take Mom to, like, the emergency ward. "Or, maybe not," she finally added.

"Lindsey! Just say yes for once," Jenna cried. "You drive me crazy!" Jenna pretended to pull out her long, straggly hair. Then another souvenir caught her eye.

"Lindsey, look at this! It's the lady in the barrel. She rolls down the Falls when you push the button." Jenna pushed a red button on the bottom of a snow globe and a barrel inside rolled down the plastic Falls, while a lady's head peeked in and out. "Buy it."

"Stop it." Gwen took the barrel lady from Jenna and put it back on the shelf. "Let's get organized. Each of us will look for a different item. Lindsey, bread; Jenna, cookies; and I'll get the meat and fruit."

"Is that a good idea?" Lindsey tucked her hair behind her ear. "I mean separating?" She loosened it and then twisted it.

"Scared?" Gwen grabbed Lindsey's hand and swung it. "Do you need me to hold your hand?"

"Whatever." Lindsey shook Gwen's hand off, holding tightly to Ginger to be sure she didn't shake her out, too. Why did Gwen do that to her all the time, make her feel so bad? "I'll find the bread." Lindsey strode down the first aisle. The right one, too. A mile of different breads stretched before her on both sides, the plastic covers shimmering in the overhead light.

Lindsey brushed her hand along the bread, feeling the plastic and the shapes. Even though they were in Canada all the bread was the same as in America. And look how many kinds there were. How was she to decide? Whichever she picked Gwen would probably say: "That's what you picked? It's so tacky." Only Gwen would say bread was tacky.

Ginger squirmed under Lindsey's coat. "Dog food!" she said to Ginger. "Forget the bread. Gwen can get that too. I'll get you some dog food, Ginger."

She switched to Aisle 4, Pet Care and Hair Products. Lindsey imagined a hair brush full of dog hair. Not appealing. She gazed at an array of dog food in as many sizes and shapes as snow globes and loaves of bread. "Ginger," she whispered to her coat. "Which one do you want?"

"How about this?" Jenna appeared around the corner waving a Canadian flag on a Popsicle stick, a red maple leaf against a white background with red borders on each side. "Will you buy this?"

"We're Americans, Jenna, aren't we?" Lindsey took it from her and looked around for a spot for it, but Lindsey didn't see a flag display.

"Where did this come from?"

"Oh, down Aisle 15."

"Aisle 15!" How had Jenna been around this entire store on those heels? Lindsey laid the flag next to a brush.

"Well, then, buy this for Mom." Jenna picked up a black velvet headband with the blue Niagara Falls logo glued on top. She jabbed at the logo. "See, it didn't peel off. It's well made. Good quality." Jenna tried it on. Her hair stuck out of the top of the headband like two devil horns. "It's positively ravishing."

"I don't know, Jenna." But this time she really did know and leaned in closer to Jenna so no one could hear. "Mom's going to lose her hair and maybe we should keep the money for—"

Jenna jerked away. "For what, Lindsey? What could we possibly spend our money on that would be better than something for Mom? She may lose her hair but this will make her pretty *now!*"

Lindsey tried to pull off the headband, but it stuck in Jenna's hair.

"Ow!" Jenna put her hands to her head. "I'm really getting irritated with you!"

Just then the kids from the hotel rushed into the store and clustered in groups around the souvenirs in the front, pushing and shoving. One boy elbowed another to get to the t-shirts. Girls screamed. "This is *so* adorable!" as they hugged the bears with the Falls embroidered on them. Lindsey tiptoed to see into the mob. Jenna jumped up and down behind her, pushing on Lindsey's shoulders to jump higher.

Lindsey pointed into the crowd. "Look, Jenna. There's Meredith. The girl who owns Ginger. Over by the cameras." She could easily make out Meredith because of her lumberjack shirt. All the other kids wore Chinowapi Choir jackets or hoodies, except for Chris, of course, who wore that great sweater.

"Really?" Jenna stopped jumping and hooted. "Meredith! Meredith!"

Meredith slipped into the crowd between a girl with jet black hair and a boy with a Chinowapi Choir jacket. Lindsey sighed in relief. Meredith hadn't seen Ginger in this condition. As if Ginger knew her real—and better—owner was near, she clawed into Lindsey stomach. Lindsey bent over and said, "Ouch," but she couldn't agree more with Ginger's unspoken comment.

"She's pretty." Jenna smiled at Lindsey. "I bet she has a nice life. I bet her mom isn't dying."

"Our mom isn't dying, Jenna. Stop that. She'll get better with all that chemo and stuff."

"I'll call her again." Jenna stretched high on her tiptoes and cupped her mouth. "Meredith! Meredith! Wherever you are, my name's Jenna. What's yours? Oh, yeah, I already know."

A few kids gawked at Jenna. She waved. "Hi."

Lindsey lifted her eyes upward and bit her lip. Jenna could be so nuts. "Stop." She tapped Jenna's hand down. "What if Chris is in there?"

"Do you want me to call the hottie too?"

"Jenna, don't you dare!" Lindsey held her breath and shook her head in vigorous little shakes.

Jenna laughed. "Oh, Lindsey. You should see your face! You must really love him. You think he's sooo adorable!"

"Oh, Jenna. You've been so exasperating this whole trip." Lindsey rubbed her forehead.

"Exasperating. You sound like Gwen. Excuse me, ah, sir. I have been, ahem, exaceperating." Jenna said this in a nasal voice and pretended to push up the bridge of a pair of glasses but slid her finger into her eye. "Ow! I'm blind." Jenna rubbed her eye enough for it to pop out.

"Serves you right." Ginger wiggled inside Lindsey's coat again, squirming against her stomach. Maybe this was how it felt to be pregnant! Lindsey opened her coat and peeked in. "Please, Gin-gin, we're in a store. I'm going to buy you some food. You like food, don't you?" Lindsey lifted her head to see one of the high school kids staring at her. She smiled and he moved on. She could imagine him saying to Chris, "I saw this one chick. She was, like, talking to her stomach. Never date her." She sure could ruin a weekend.

"Jenna, Ginger's restless. Do you think it is alright to keep her in here so long? She's damp, too, steaming up a sauna on my stomach."

"Take her out." Jenna threw her arms out. "Simple solution to a simple problem."

"Do you think so? French people let dogs go everywhere but do Canadians? I mean they speak French so does that make them French about their dogs? You know, Jenna, I haven't heard any French. Have you?"

Without answering, Jenna grabbed Ginger from under Lindsey's coat. Lindsey struggled to hold on to her but Ginger wiggled and wiggled, her tail practically generating heat in her desperation to be free.

"Your Mommies won't let you go," Jenna said as they both clung to her.

"Hey, Lisa O'Day. Great to see you!" Meredith slapped Lindsey on the back. Lindsey lurched forward, and Ginger dropped to the ground. Ginger barked and barked in her new freedom.

"Ginger's loose!" Meredith cried. "Quick! Hide her or someone will see!" Meredith paced and gestured with her hands as if making a speech. "Now I'll never sing a solo. I'm doomed. The world is over." Meredith's face broke out in blotches, and her eyes watered. Lindsey couldn't believe it, but tough old Meredith might cry. Ginger jumped on Lindsey's leg and yipped as if yelling at Lindsey too.

Gwen approached with a bag of apples and lunch meat in her hands. "Look at the great deals I found." Gwen hefted up the bag of apples. "Two fifty Canadian."

Meredith stopped gesturing and tilted her head slightly, squinting at Gwen, while Ginger barked at Gwen, her tail wagging furiously.

"Hey, what is that dog doing out?" Gwen asked. "You can't let a dog out in a grocery store. Are you trying to get us arrested?"

Meredith placed her hand on her heart. "Arrested? You mean you can get arrested for this? Man! This is nuts. It's straight horrible. I'm doomed."

"Meredith, I don't think you'll get arrested," Lindsey said. "In *Tamera Wins the Day*, she carried her dog in Lacy's department store and no one called the police; they even sold her a bottle of Love's Passion perfume."

"Nobody cares about your dumb old books," Gwen said.

Ginger growled at her and then scurried down the aisle.

"Ginger is getting away!" Lindsey yelled.

Marcus and Chris appeared around the corner.

"Hey, there's a dog loose in here." Chris pointed down the aisle. "Is it yours?" he asked Gwen, not noticing Lindsey. Lindsey quickly hid his hat in her pocket. She patted it down but it looked like she'd shoplifted a snow globe.

"Oh, yes, could you help me?" Gwen blushed and smoothed the blonde streak in her hair. "I'm so upset. It was so silly of me to let my little doggy loose. Would you help me look down this aisle?"

Marcus and Chris bowed and said, "Glad to be of service."

"I'd tip my hat," Chris joked. "Only it's been stolen. Shall we?" They linked elbows and headed down the aisle like Dorothy and her pals down the yellow brick road. "Excelsior!"

Jenna sashayed after them. Gwen whipped around and gave her the evil eye, and mouthed, "Go away!" Jenna wobbled back.

"Your sister knows Marcus and Chris? They're, like, the most popular guys in school."

"She didn't, but it looks like she does now." Lindsey continued to watch them go down the aisle, Gwen laughing, flirting, and flipping her hair.

"I planned to go to your hotel room with this dog food." Meredith held up a bag covered in quarter-sized gold sequins. "And tell you something that I should have—"

"I'll carry that." Jenna snatched the bag from Meredith. "This is one sweet bag," she added looking inside.

"Yeah, my mom gave it to me. She's always trying to give me girlie things."

"Um, shouldn't we look for Ginger?" Lindsey asked.

"Yeah, maybe hottie Chris and Gwen will be too busy kissing." Jenna covered her hand in kisses. Lindsey shoved her and Jenna toppled over. "Better watch it, Missy," Jenna said as she stood back up and stared Lindsey down. "I may get mad at you and you never like that." Lindsey opened her eyes wide and stared back, tilting her head.

"Please, Lindsey, do something!" A wrinkle appeared between Meredith's eyes. "Didn't you get it? If Doctor Schwab finds Ginger, I'm toast. I'm out of the choir. I'm sent home. I'm ruined." Meredith put her hands on Lindsey's shoulders and shook them. "You gotta help me. It's why I gave Ginger to you in the first place." Meredith dropped her hands. "I mean, please. Get me out of this mess—this kerfuffle."

Lindsey could fell her heart clinch and shrivel at the idea of being in charge but her friend was counting on her. It's what Annie Edison Taylor, the barrel lady, would do—take charge—face danger, even danger like Doctor Schwab. Lindsey imagined herself in a barrel, protected only by a thin mattress, barreling through the Food Lion after Ginger, barreling over Doctor Schwab with Gwen in her pursuit. Yes, she could!

"Come on then!" Lindsey dragged Jenna toward the front of the store and Meredith followed. "We can do it. We'll rescue her."

They spun around a corner and straight into Doctor Schwab, Lindsey bumping into her shoulder.

"Young ladies." Doctor Schwab rubbed the shoulder. "Please slow down."

"Sorry, Dr. Schwab." Lindsey walked around her, dragging Jenna who dragged Meredith like a game of crack the whip.

Doctor Schwab held out her hand for them to stop. "Miss Burke, I see you've found your roommate again. Hello, Miss Lisa O'Day."

"Yes," Meredith answered. "I thought she'd left, but she came back,"

"And who is this young lady in the unfortunate choice of shoes?" Doctor Schwab frowned at Jenna.

"I'm Jenna. My mom is sick." Jenna held up the sequined bag. "This bag has her medicine. Are you a real doctor? Can you help her?"

"Oh, my." Doctor Schwab patted her hand over her heart. "I wish I was a doctor to help your mom but I'm a doctor of child psychology."

"Oh, you're a doctor of that. Too bad. I wanted to buy my mom this." Jenna showed Doctor Schwab the headband. "But Lind, I mean Lisa, and Meredith wouldn't help me. I don't have any money. We're too poor. Poor and sick." Jenna hung her head and let her hair droop in front of her. Lindsey couldn't believe the things Jenna said, but it sure was melting Doctor Schwab. Meredith and Lindsey inched away.

"You are a sweet child." Doctor Schwab brushed the velvet of the headband and picked off a piece of lint. "Doctor Schwab thinks you are a girl to be commended." She glared at Meredith and Lindsey who stopped moving and smiled. "What does your mother have?"

"She has not-Rodgers."

"Not-Rodgers? Doctor Schwab has never heard of that."

Lindsey heard the clip of nails on the floor. It must be Ginger! She strained her neck to see down the aisle, Aisle 5, but snapped it back when Doctor Schwab said:

"I hope you girls are paying attention to this young lady's tale of woe."

Lindsey and Meredith nodded.

"Let Doctor Schwab buy that headband for you, Jenna. Come with me to the cashier." As Jenna wobbled alongside of her, Doctor Schwab stopped. "Doctor Schwab thinks those are very inappropriate shoes for a young lady."

"It's the only shoes we could afford. I had to wear my mother's."

"Oh, you poor, poor thing." Doctor Schwab cradled Jenna's face in her hands. "Doctor Schwab will buy you a pair. Come with me."

Whew, Lindsey hadn't had to do a thing to get rid of Doctor Schwab; Jenna had done it all. But had she done it to help them, or just to get a headband? Oh, well, it didn't matter. Doctor Schwab was off their scent. Lindsey motioned to Meredith and they hurried down Aisle 5: Laundry Detergent and Cleaning Products, but Ginger was long gone, leaving no canine clues.

At the end of the aisle, they entered a wide area with wagons set up with different Christmas-themed souvenirs: Santa riding a sleigh down the frozen water; stuffed reindeer and zebras; fairies; nothing that would interest a dog. Along the other side of the wagons stood mini stores: a Jim Thorton's, a pet store, and a candle store (who knew, maybe they sold candles that smelled like the Falls!). Lindsey's eyes grew wide. The Food Lion went on forever.

"Where should we go, Lindsey?" Meredith waited like a dog waited for a treat. How was she to figure out where Ginger was? Hadn't Meredith noticed what a huge conglomeration of stores this was?

Meredith hit Lindsey on the arm and pointed toward the deli. "Look! Can you believe that? It's terrible! Horrible! A disaster."

CATCHING THE LION

What? What was terrible, a disaster? Was Ginger lying hurt? Had she caused Ginger's death? A pain shot through Lindsey all the way to her stomach as she visualized Ginger lying under a Christmas wagon, her tongue hanging out, her eyes staring straight ahead with X's in them, her tummy bulging. Lindsey stooped to peer under the wagons but there was nothing but dust balls and long lost Jim Thorton's cups.

"No, silly." Meredith tapped her on her shoulder and Lindsey stood up. "They're not under there. They're over there at Jim Thornton's. Your sister's drinking a Coke with Chris and Marcus. I guess Jenna was right. They aren't looking too hard. It's why I knew I could only count on you."

Gwen sat on a high stool at a counter laughing and pulling on her blonde streak, as she sipped her Coke through a straw. She swiveled to talk to Marcus and then swiveled to talk to Chris. Gwen could have been in a 1950's beach movie. Tamera hadn't even done that in *Tamera's Two Dates*. Nuts if she was going to watch her sister steal away her … her …

well, her crush. No, she'd concentrate on finding Ginger and succeeding for once. No fear. Meredith thought she could do it and so she could.

Now, to do some detective work. Where would a dog go? Lindsey spun around. Yes, that was it.

"Let's go *there*." She pointed to a red *Meats* sign.

"Great idea." Meredith slapped Lindsey on the back. "I'm with you all the way, kid." Meredith followed closely behind Lindsey to the meat section, so closely that Lindsey could hear her sniffle. Lindsey skidded to a stop, causing Meredith to crash into her.

"Ouch! This is a dangerous mission." Meredith rubbed her stomach. "I bruise easily, you know."

"Sorry, but look! Ginger's by the meat!" Ginger stood on her hind legs yipping and scratching at the meat counter, her round belly sagging. Luckily for the store but not for Ginger, the meat was enclosed in glass with plastic green grass surrounding each slab. Red Canadian flags flew overhead, and maple leafs decorated the glass. Stacks of mustards jars and sauces surrounded the counter like a fortress.

The butcher with his wide belly wrapped in white apron measured a stack of pork chops for a lady wearing a black scarf, gray raincoat, and large dark glasses that hid her face. Ginger moved closer to the lady, yipping at her. Oh, no! Ginger bumped the stack of mustard jars. They tumbled across the floor, spilling a stream of yellow scum. It startled Ginger, and she yipped and raced away.

"Ah!" the lady cried and staggered against the counter as if wounded. "It's a rat! There's a rat in the store. A filthy, horrid rat! Get the manager! Get the Health Department! Get the ambulance! I'm fainting!"

"There are no rats in here!" the butcher slammed the pork chops on the counter. "I keep my store clean!" He ran his finger along the top of the glass and waved his finger in her face.

"Do not talk back to me, young man." The lady stomped her foot. "I know what I saw. How do you think these jars tipped over? Its pink nose stared right up at me." She pointed her two fingers at her eyes. "Right at me. Throw those pork chops away and escort me to the police." At that, several men in dark suits approached her.

"May we help you, ma'am? What seems to be the trouble?" one of the men with gray hair said. "I'm the store manager." He wore a lavender tie and blue shirt.

Lindsey stopped listening when Meredith whispered in her ear, "Should we clean up the mustard?"

"Hmm." Lindsey twisted her hair. "No." She shook her head as the lady screamed more hysterically, "Rat! Rat!" and three more managers surrounded her. "We better catch Ginger and keep her from causing more trouble."

Meredith nodded. "Good thinking."

Ginger had moved to the fish counter, and now licked a pea-soup-like goop in a wide puddle on the floor. Blech. It kept her occupied at least. She didn't jump up on the jars of seafood sauces that were stacked in front of the fish.

"Come on." Lindsey waved for Meredith to follow her. Meredith started to say something but Lindsey placed her finger on her lips and shushed her. "Slow and quiet. We'll nab her when we get closer." Meredith nodded in agreement and together they tiptoed toward Ginger like they were sneaking downstairs to see presents on Christmas Eve.

The closer they got, the clearer Lindsey could see Ginger's red tongue move in and out, in and out licking the green goop, her bow dripping in it. Excuse me, she said to herself, but Ginger did *not* look like a rat. She could smell the fish now and see the great white and red slabs of it lying in beds of ice with their bones showing through. She read signs for Sea Bass and Salmon, with the French names under them: *de bar, de saumon*. Over the counter hung a picture of a cow and pig saying, *Eat Fish*.

"It working," Meredith said in a whisper. "We're close!"

"Yes." Lindsey nodded. A thrill shot through her. It felt good to be in control and solving a problem, not Gwen. Her moment of glory.

"Let's nab her," Meredith said when they were about three feet from Ginger. "Should we nab her?"

"No, we need to get closer and get her attention without anyone hearing us." When Lindsey said that, Ginger stopped eating and perked her ears, searching around. Was she going to run away? No, her little tongue snuck back out and she licked away at the green goop.

"Think, Lindsey!" Meredith cried. "I don't want to leave choir! Not before I get a chance to sing solo!"

"I got it!" Lindsey dragged Meredith behind a display of pumpkin pie cans. "Let's buy meat and dangle it in front of her. She'll stop eating that gross goop and follow us. We'll trap her with meat kindness."

"Meat kindness. That's funny." Meredith held her hand up for a high five. Lindsey hit it. "Ow!" Meredith shook her hand out. "Remember I bruise easily."

"Sorry." Meredith looked so tough in her lumberjack outfit, Lindsey forgot she was a wuss.

"So, what'll we do for money?" Meredith turned the pockets of her jeans inside out. "I already spent mine on a Jim Thornton's Double Doubles. I *love* my coffee! We should buy salami. Ginger *loves* salami."

Lindsey tugged her wad of money from her coat pocket, her pocket turning inside out showing a hole. She stuffed the pocket back in before Meredith noticed but she didn't need to worry because Meredith eyeballed the money practically drooling.

"Cool! Jenna said you guys were poor." Meredith yanked a $20 off of the top. She examined it. "It's American. They'll charge extra to spend American here, but that won't matter."

Won't matter to whom? Lindsey wondered.

"Stay here and keep an eye on Ginger while I rendezvous for zee salami." Meredith winked. "I speak zee French alzoo." She headed to the deli counter. An over-sized lady in a pink pantsuit squeezed in front of her and placed her order for, "Five pounds of turkey, sliced extra fine." Meredith whipped around and shrugged at Lindsey and Lindsey shrugged back. She would have liked to have executed her own plan, but oh, well. She was so nervous, her hand shook. The same nervousness when it was her turn in a spelling bee—the churning in her stomach like she'd switched on a blender.

In front of her, cans of pumpkin pie filling with pictures of pie topped with whipped cream lined the shelves. One side was written in French and the other in American. Funny how she hadn't met anyone who spoke French yet. She read the labels for calories. The French in France weren't fat but were the French in Canada?

Ahhh—what was that? Meredith slapped a white package as thin as an envelope on Lindsey's back and snuck behind the pumpkin pie display with her.

"Lucky, they had Ginger's favorite." Meredith smiled. "Only the best."

Lindsey tilted her head to read the price on the white package. $6.00! Oh, bother! That was more than they'd paid for her omelet. She should have stayed in control of this project.

Meredith peeled off a slice of salami. Lindsey inhaled the husky smell of garlic and spices. Her mouth watered as if she'd turned on a faucet. It had been ages since breakfast. Meredith bit off a piece and nibbled around the entire slice. "To take off the skin so Ginger doesn't choke," she said with a strand of salami dangling from her mouth.

"We better hurry." Lindsey took charge again. "Whatever Ginger is licking up could make her sick." Meredith nodded and handed her a slice of salami.

"Gin, Gin!" They waved and wiggled their salami at Ginger from behind their hiding place.

Ginger started toward Meredith, then stopped and panted.

"Maybe we should creep in closer," Lindsey said in a whisper. "But then again, maybe we should just jump out and surprise her ... but no, wait ..."

"Let's go then!" Meredith dragged Lindsey from behind the display calling, "Ginger! Come to Mommy!"

Jenna and Doctor Schwab appeared in front of Ginger. Meredith collided into Jenna, who knocked into Lindsey and sent her spinning through the green goop and into the display of pumpkin pie cans. As Lindsey spun around, Ginger gulped a doggie treat from a bin, trotted down Aisle 10, and wagged her tail goodbye.

"My shoes!" Jenna cried from where she'd collapsed in a puddle of goop. "Look at my beautiful shoes! They're ruined." She shook them, sending flecks of goop flying into Lindsey's hair. Lindsey stared back in disbelief and Meredith let out a wail, "Wah!"

"Was that a dog I saw?" Doctor Schwab cried. "A dog in the store! Doctor Schwab is sure she saw a dog in the store." At that, the lady with the raincoat strode over from where she stood with the managers.

"A rat." The lady shook her head at Dr. Schwab. "Tell Doctor Schwab that he saw a rat."

"*I'm* Doctor Schwab," Doctor Schwab said in disgust as she picked up Jenna and glared at Lindsey and Meredith on the floor. "And *I* saw a dog."

"Well, you must be blind." The lady stomped her foot. "It was a rat!"

"How dare you?" Doctor Schwab stood a little taller and flared her nostrils.

Lindsey glanced at Meredith, and they both laughed. They stuffed the rest of the salami in their mouths, still sitting in the goop. "We didn't see a dog, Doctor Schwab!" A wad of salami protruded from Meredith's mouth, and she choked it back in.

"It's not funny!" Jenna shook her fists at them. "Look what you did to my shoes!"

"You see," the lady in the raincoat said. "They didn't see a dog—they saw a rat!"

"We didn't see a rat either," Meredith said and Lindsey shook her head in agreement.

"Ignore those two ruffians." Doctor Schwab waved her hand across Meredith and Lindsey. "They know nothing. Look at them, eating meat. They're quite disgusting."

A store manager appeared behind the lady in the raincoat. He stared down at the mess and called on his walkie-talkie, "Clean up on Aisle 10!" Then he said to the lady, "Now, ma'am, we would like to offer you a $50 gift card for your—"

"You will not get me out of here with bribery!" The lady flailed her arms at the manager. "I saw a rat. I want justice!" If the lady only had an umbrella to go with her raincoat, she surely would have hit the man over the head with it.

Doctor Schwab ignored the lady and the manager, and said to Meredith, "Miss Burke, I believe you were hoping to be one of the soloists?" Meredith stopped chewing and nodded, her eyes wide and sad.

"Well, Mr. Kleptomanie will hear about your antics." Doctor Schwab rose on her toes, inhaled deeply, and blew down hard on a whistle around her neck. A second later, Walter, the Hagrid look-alike, stormed over.

"For Pete's sake, Schwab. I told you never to blow that thing. Give it to me." He held out his hand and Dr. Schwab relinquished it. "Now, what's wrong?"

"I saw a rat!" the lady in the raincoat said.

Walter stared in disbelief. "You called me to tell me this lady saw a rat, Schwab?" He spun back around on his heels to leave.

Doctor Schwab tapped him on the shoulder. He turned back and she gazed at him with stars in her eyes—definitely stars. "Remember, you can call me Wilma," she said. Lindsey almost thought Doctor Schwab was going to bat her eyes at him. Doctor Schwab had a crush on Walter! It made Lindsey giggle. If only she could tell Jenna.

"What do you want, Schwab?"

Doctor Schwab cleared her throat. "I called you because these girls have been misbehaving." She pointed to Lindsey and Meredith.

Lindsey and Meredith struggled up. Meredith slipped in the goop and used Lindsey to steady herself. She said in a whisper, "You look terrible, Lisa. You should see your hair."

Lindsey touched her hair. Ah, green goop. Gross. She gagged. She prayed it was soup, and not something really toxic, like, well, like who knew!

"Yes, Meredith is in the choir." Walter said. "But I don't remember this young lady in our choir." Walter scratched his head. "I do remember her on the boy's floor this morning."

"Miss O'Day was on the boy's floor?" Doctor Schwab shot her hand in the air. "She shall be expelled."

"Miss O'Day? I thought Miss O'Day was tall and an alto." Walter scratched his head. "I'm puzzled."

Jenna shook Lindsey's arm. "Tell her."

Lindsey nodded. "I can't be expelled, Doctor Schwab, because—"

"Doctor Schwab says you *can*." She slammed her hand down to her side.

Lindsey nodded in agreement. Forget it. Doctor Schwab was never going to listen. Let her expel her.

"Now, Walter, as you recall, Miss Burke asked to audition for a solo. I believe based on the rules, she is now disqualified from all participation in the choir, including singing at the Falls or trying out for the solo."

"Disqualified from all participation?" Walter pulled on his beard. "That seems harsh when all she's done is slip in this green goop."

She looked at him with googly eyes. Walter didn't seem to notice so she said. "Section 12 of the school bylaws says that you are banned from participating in all extracurricular activities when caught misbehaving." Doctor Schwab pulled a black manual with worn edges from her fanny pack. She riffled through it to a page highlighted entirely in yellow. "Page 37." She handed it to Walter.

He shook his head and didn't take it. "They look like they've been punished enough."

Meredith frowned and shivered starting at her toes and finishing with her head. She sneezed. "I catch colds easily."

Walter tugged off his Chinowapi hoodie and handed it to Meredith. She dragged a sleeve in the goop as she put it on. "How about if we leave it that Miss Burke just doesn't try out for the solo?"

Meredith opened her mouth and then shut it. Her head slowly tilted to the ground, until it hung low, heavy, and sad. Jenna rubbed Meredith's arm. Meredith didn't look up. Meredith had told her this was going to happen. Lindsey knew she should say something, but what? Doctor Schwab never listened.

Lindsey felt a hand helping her up and turned to see Gwen. "What kind of mess are you in?" she hissed. Chris and Marcus stood behind, with Marcus carrying Ginger. Oh, wonderful. Ginger was safe! What a relief, but oh, what Chris must think of her. She pulled her hair, stiff with goop, in front of her face so he wouldn't recognize her.

"Hey, it's you!" Chris pointed his finger at her. "Give me my hat."

"Did you see it too, young man?" The lady in the raincoat crossed over the goop to Chris. "Did you see the rat?"

"No, my hat. That girl has my hat and my ears are cold."

"Now, ma'am, I must ask you to be careful not to disparage the store," the manager said, with an exasperated tone. "Really, now I have a $100 gift card—"

"We need to get out of here," Gwen said. "The problems of your kooky friend with the dog aren't ours." Gwen took Ginger from Marcus. "Thanks," she smiled as sweetly as Doctor Schwab had at Walter. Then she thrust the dog at Lindsey. "Give the stupid dog back to the kooky girl, now!" she hissed.

"No!" Lindsey hissed back and wrapped Ginger in her coat. "She'll get in more trouble!"

"You're an idiot." Gwen said. "I want out of here." She grabbed Jenna's hand. Jenna gaped at Gwen for a second then snapped to attention when Gwen's eyes stabbed into her.

"My sister is here, Wilma!" Jenna waved. "Bye and thanks for the headband."

"Oh, goodbye, dear." Doctor Schwab waved as Jenna hobbled to the front of the store.

Lindsey took off too.

Doctor Schwab called after her, "Miss O'Day! Where are you going?"

Then the lady in the raincoat cried, "They must have seen the rat. That's why they're leaving. Everyone, leave the store! Evacuate! Rat Infestation!"

LOSING HEART

Outside the sky had turned a murky purple black. Crowds of people roamed the streets, bumping into the girls, mostly families laughing, bundled in scarves and hats, mothers pushing strollers, fathers carrying toddlers, their breath hanging in the air. The neon lights of restaurants flashed, inviting them in for a nice meal. Some restaurants called out their specials, "$15.99 all-you-can-eat ribs!" Lindsey's stomach growled. All the people headed down the hill, while she and her sisters trudged upward against the wind, to the poor side of town. Her mucky hair froze in the blasts of wind.

"What time is it?" Jenna asked looking into the sky. "Does it get dark sooner in Canada?" Her long black hair whipped around her, obscuring her face.

"No, a storm's coming," Gwen said, her face tucked downward against the wind.

"Oh, look, way over there, at that Ferris wheel." Jenna pointed to a luminescent white Ferris wheel with glass gondolas circling in the air, like a spinning chrysanthemum with water droplets. "It's awesome."

"I read about it in a guidebook," Gwen said. "It's called the SkyWheel. It's taller than the Statue of Liberty. You only think it's close because it is so big. It's way over by the wax museum on Clifton Hill, where all the tacky stuff is."

Lindsey wondered what could be tackier than the stuff *they* were passing: tattoo and body piercing shop, parking lots ($5 a day), a wax museum of famous criminals painted white with black images of criminals running across the front. Their side of town celebrated criminals, not celebrities.

"I want to ride it," Jenna demanded. "That would be even better than the wax museum."

"We can't go now." Gwen tightened her coat against an angry gust of wind that rushed passed them and down the hill. "We're late enough already. Besides I read that it's expensive. Mom only has money for the wax museum."

"Lindsey has money, don't you, Lindsey?" Jenna ran backward in front of Lindsey. "You didn't have to buy Ginger dog food so you still have lots."

"Well, I don't know." Lindsey thought of the $6 that Meredith had spent on the salami. "I mean maybe Gwen's right. Look how dark it is."

"Take me! Take me!" Jenna cried.

"Oh, Jenna, I don't know."

"You never know, Lindsey. I hate you," Jenna said. "You won't live with me while Mom is sick. You won't buy me anything. You didn't even help Meredith when she was punished and couldn't have a solo."

"Cross now!" Gwen yelled and they scurried to the other side. "Hurry! Cars!"

Jenna heels caught in a pothole and she stumbled. A car screeched around her.

"Jenna! Let me help you up!" Lindsey ran toward her and offered her free hand.

"No, I can get up. I don't need you." Jenna pushed up on her hands and crab walked across.

"Didn't Doctor Schwab buy you new shoes?" Lindsey asked following beside her.

"No, Doctor Schwab didn't buy me shoes." Jenna straightened with dignity. "What do you think I am? Someone who begs for free shoes?"

Icy sleet hit Lindsey's forehead. She looked up in the sky and sleet plopped in her eye.

"Run!" Gwen took off up the hill.

Lindsey could see their hotel a block away. Its yellow brick mingling with the sleet and the yellow arrow pointing to the left flashing "$5 Parking."

"Ginger has to go!" Lindsey called after her. "Don't leave me behind."

"I don't care. I'm not stopping. It's your problem. Come on, Jenna!"

Jenna walked backward. "I gotta stay with Gwen!"

"At least give me Meredith's bag!"

Jenna ran back and handed it to her. "Probably a lot of cool stuff in there." Jenna looked wistfully at the sequined bag as the wind whipped it sideways.

"I've got to find a leash." Lindsey tried to hold the bag steady in the blowing wind.

"Bye!" Jenna ran to the hotel.

Lindsey dropped to her knees onto the now deserted sidewalk. The wind and the rain screeched around her. Her hair dripped into the bag as she searched it for a leash. She pulled out a leash, scattering the remaining contents on the sidewalk. The leash, made of burnished silver, flashed in the dark. Just like Tamera would have had but no time to admire it. She shoved the other contents back in the bag, and hooked the leash on Ginger's collar. Ginger's little feet skittered to the grass where she squatted.

"Oh, no!" Lindsey smashed her hand against her forehead. "What do I do now?"

"Stoop and scoop." Jenna and Gwen stood next to her, sleet streaming down their coats.

"With what?" She stared down at Chris' empty hat, soaked from the sleet. "This?"

They nodded.

Lindsey scooped Ginger's gift into Chris' hat and tucked Ginger under her coat. She held firm so Ginger wouldn't have a bumpy ride. Bumpy ride. That's what Lindsey certainly was having. She needed a mattress to soften her fall, like Annie, the barrel lady, but Annie wasn't running to a ramshackle hotel with unmentionables in a boy's hat after having deserted a friend.

Minutes later, Mom held the door for them. "You girls are soaked."

"It's raining and sleeting—nasty out." Gwen and Jenna shook their wet hair at each other. Lindsey only hoped the sleet had washed the goop from hers.

Mom parted the curtains and peered out. Sleet crisscrossed the window, blocking the view of the square box hotels across the street and the sign of the parking lot flashing $5. "No Falls tonight, girls." She smiled her watery smile. "I'd better not risk getting wet. But we can do something fun in the hotel, and have our picnic."

"I gotta go." Gwen dropped the groceries on the floor, and the apples rolled out. In the harsh light, Lindsey could see the wrinkles on them— *they* were in need of Botox. Mom picked up and inspected one. She placed it on the kitchen table.

"They were only 2.50 Canadian," Gwen said. "I made a good purchase. So, like I was saying, I'm going to use the computer in the lobby to e-mail a friend."

Right, thought Lindsey, a friend whose name was Chris.

"But you're wet. And what about our picnic?" Mom asked.

"I'll be back in a few." Gwen slammed the door behind her.

"Lindsey, what do you have in your coat?" Mom asked. "You girls don't think we're so poor that we have to steal?" She rubbed her forehead and headed back to the bed.

"No, it's just my hat. I didn't want it to get wet." Add that to her list: lying to Mom. But at least Mom hadn't noticed the green goop that had splashed the entire side of her coat, drying to a pale silver. Add hiding goop to her list of lies.

Jenna lunged for the bed next to Mom. Lindsey snuck behind the upright cover of her suitcase, pulling the sequined bag along with her. She snuck Ginger out of coat and under a towel. Ginger snuggled happily into the towels, digging in to Gwen's pink sweater.

She stretched out her belly and Lindsey swore it wiggled. That was some chubby fat. She fed Ginger doggie kibbles from her hand that she'd found in the sequined bag. Then she headed to the bathroom to dispose of Ginger's droppings.

When she returned, Jenna grabbed the headband from a Food Lion bag. "I forgot, Mom. A nice lady helped me buy this for you."

"It's beautiful." She hugged Jenna and tried on the headband, smiling into the mirror. "It'll help me remember this trip always."

"I don't want to remember the trip." Jenna bounced down, and up bounced Mom. "It's been terrible. Simply the most horrible day of my life. I'm freaked about it. I've been psychologically damaged." Jenna buried her head in the pillow.

"Jenna, what's wrong?" Mom patted Jenna's hair. "By goodness, what's in your hair?"

Jenna flipped over and said, "I told you. I had the most horrible day. Look at my shoes!" Jenna tilted her shoes to best show off the green stains, like someone had thrown up on them. Was she going to snitch and tell about the store and the SkyWheel?

"How did this happen?" Mom spread her arms across the bed. "Can't you girls even go to a store a block away without trouble?"

"Lindsey knocked me into sea-green, oozy toxic waste at the Food Lion." Jenna sat up and glared at Lindsey who snuck back behind the upright suitcase. "Poisonous vapors rose from it! I was horrified." Jenna shuddered. "It's difficult for me to think about." She swiped the back of her hand across her forehead.

"Lindsey! Did you do this?" Mom sat up. "Let me see you." Lindsey sighed and stood, the suitcase hiding most of the goop on her coat. "Why look at you! You're a worse mess."

"It was an accident." Lindsey twisted her hair behind her ear. "Wasn't it, Jenna?"

"Do you hear someone, Mother?" Jenna crawled off the bed and to the T.V. "I thought I heard something evil in the wind."

"But, Jenna, it was your fault too," Lindsey said. "You stepped in the way!"

"Yes, Mother, that definitely is the sound that something evil makes."

Mom's anger in her eyes faded to sadness. She walked to the window. Lindsey should tell Mom everything. If she was getting punished, she might as well get it all over at once. Nervous to know what Mom might do, Lindsey wandered over to the T.V. and switched it on. The hotel channel announced, "Please use the Wi-Fi lounge in the lobby for free Wi-Fi access." She increased the volume to drown out her own thoughts.

"That's as loud as the evil one will be allowed to make it." Lindsey heard Jenna say as she appeared at her side and wrestled the remote from her and switched off the T.V.

Lindsey let Jenna have it and moved to the kitchen. Mom still looked out the window. Lindsey made a deal with herself. When Mom said something, she'd tell her. Yep. Tell her everything. Lindsey twisted the knobs of the burners, watching the burners glow red against the white of the stove, magnifying the black scratches in the enamel. The far back left burner only partially glowed like a half moon so she twisted the knob off and back on. Out of the corner of her eye, she noticed Jenna sneaking behind her. Jenna reached across her and twisted all the burners off.

Lindsey took a second to think of where to go next, but Jenna thought quicker and chased her to the fireplace and flipped it on. The fireplace flickered to life, flaring up but never consuming the logs guarded behind the gold screen. Lindsey flipped it off.

"Stop it! I can't stand this bickering!" Mom turned from the window. "It has to stop!" A mark on her forehead glowed red where she'd leaned against the cold window.

"It's never me, Mother." Jenna fell back on the bed in exasperation. "It's the other girls."

Lindsey couldn't stop roaming, thinking what she'd say to her, "Well, Mom, I took a hat from a boy, took a dog from a girl, and took a solo from a friend. Oh, and Jenna's steaming mad at me."

She opened the refrigerator. Bare wire shelves stared back at her. Nothing in it but skinny ice cubes and a musty odor. The refrigerator light didn't even work. She reached for an ice cube. Jenna hopped up and shut the refrigerator door, giving Lindsey only time to slide her hand out and scoop the ice cube in her mouth. Yuck! She spat it out. It tasted stale!

"For heaven's sake. I no longer care what happened." Mom crawled under covers. "Jenna, take a shower. Lindsey, you help her."

"Didn't I make that clear?" Jenna put her hands on her nonexistent hips. "I'm not speaking to Lindsey. And, Mother, I can certainly navigate the shower. I am not a child. I believe, if I'm not mistaken, that Miss Lindsey already showed us how to turn it on. You might want to ask her about it and several other things while I'm refreshing myself from the terrors of the day." Jenna lifted her head in the air, as if her only purpose was to hold her nose high, and headed for the bathroom.

"Alright, Jenna," Mom said. "Go figure it out yourself. And, Lindsey, clean up that suitcase. I'm not telling you again." Mom faced the wall.

"OK." Lindsey snuck back behind the suitcase and moved the towels around a bit. She let Ginger lick the ice cube. She opened the picture book about Annie. A good choice but Lindsey let it drop. Annie had courage, not Lindsey. She sat in Niagara Falls behind a suitcase! When she thought of Mom's sickness, her decision, Gwen and Chris, Jenna hating her, and Meredith not getting a chance at a solo, the tears flowed. She didn't even want to remember Meredith's face when she'd left her alone with the true incarnation of evil, Doctor Schwab. She stuffed the end of a towel in her mouth so Jenna and Mom couldn't hear her. She gagged. Dumb idea, like everything she did.

"Ah," called Jenna from the shower.

Lindsey looked up and met Mom's eye.

"I don't have a towel!" Jenna cried.

A while later, back behind the suitcase, after her turn in the shower, where she'd scrubbed her coat clean of the toxic goop, Jenna complained to Lindsey, "I can't believe you took all the towels." Jenna applied black nail polish to Mom's big toe.

"Yes, why *do* you have so many towels, Lindsey?" Mom wiped a glob of black polish from her foot. She tilted her foot back and forth, a crease forming between her eyes.

"You should make her take them back," Jenna said. "I know she doesn't need them." Jenna grabbed Mom's foot. "You have to hold your foot still or this isn't going to look good."

Lindsey opened her mouth to think of an answer, but a knock on the door saved her.

Jenna dropped the polish on the beige carpet, a black drop invading the beige world. "Somebody's at the door! Maybe it's the house detective.

Maybe he's after a *dog*!" She spun to glare at Lindsey. Could she be right? Are there house detectives? And would they know about her dog?

"Oh, Jenna, you watch too many old movies," Mom answered. "I doubt hotels have detectives anymore."

Whew, Mom had to be right. She was getting as paranoid as Meredith. Maybe it was a curly haired hottie whose name might be Chris, who was tired of Gwen's dreary and dull email and was looking for his baby-soft hat. What would she do? Laugh and say, "Oh, you wouldn't believe what happened." And, he'd laugh and they'd laugh together. No, she'd probably say something dumb and he would laugh at that. Besides it was Gwen. At that, Lindsey had an idea. She'd win Jenna back by banding together against Gwen like they always did!

She jumped out from behind her suitcase. "Come on, Jenna. Let's not let Gwen in. Let's play a joke."

"That is so childish of you, Lindsey," Jenna said. "No wonder I'm not speaking to you. My hatred for you is boiling to the surface."

Lindsey crawled back to the suitcase and her misery.

"Come in, Gwendolyn," Jenna called, cupping her hands. Gwen pounded harder. Jenna addressed Mom. "This hotel isn't that good. Gwen ought to be careful or she'll break down the door."

"Open it, Jenna," Mom said.

"Yes, I must put a halt to my infuriated sister's destruction," Jenna said.

Jenna opened the door and Gwen stormed in. "Took you, like, forever to let me in, you little creep."

"Hello, to you, too, Gwendolyn." Jenna returned to polishing Mom's fingernails, this time purple. Lindsey's heart squeezed as Jenna so comfortably made Mom happy.

"Are you sure this purple goes with the black toenails?" Mom pursed her lips.

"Oh." Jenna inspected them. "Maybe you're right. I could paint one finger purple and the next black—a checkerboard!"

"No, that's alright." Mom shook her head. "Go ahead the way you were."

Jenna stayed calm. Her storm over, Lindsey could talk to her. Explain how everything had happened. Lindsey felt lighter at the thought. Talking to Jenna always put things into their simplest ways.

"Jenna—"

Gwen shook Lindsey's shoulder hard.

"Stop it, Gwen." Lindsey wiggled away. "That hurt."

"Girls," Mom said. "Just a little peace before our picnic, please."

Gwen knelt next to Lindsey by the suitcase. "I had to get your attention away from those books." Lindsey could feel her breath on her cheek. Yuckier than the ice cube.

"I want to be included." Jenna rested her chin on Gwen's shoulder. "I'm a gossip queen too. Is it about the hottie?"

Gwen stared at her and squinted.

"Or maybe I don't." She slunk back to Mom and applied purple polish to Mom's last finger.

"The kids from the high school are a choir," Gwen continued in a whisper to Lindsey. "After their choir practice tonight, they're hosting a pizza party and then skating at the Rink at the Brink. I want to go with them."

"So, what do I care?" Lindsey picked up the book and pretended to read. She knew that all Gwen wanted was to be with Chris.

"They still think you're one of them so if you go, I can go. No one will notice."

"*I* should go with *you*?" Lindsey raised her voice.

Jenna and Mom looked over at them.

"Is something wrong, girls?" Mom asked.

"No, Mother. All's well." Gwen shifted back to Lindsey. "Quiet! I only want you because I need you, believe me. So, here's the deal. If you don't go, I'll tell Mom that you took that rat dog *and* Chris' hat *and* that you made the mess at the Food Lion. After the picnic, we'll say we're going to the look around the hotel and then go." Gwen held out her hand to shake. "Deal?"

So this is how it felt to be blackmailed? Lindsey studied Gwen's sharp green eyes. Had Tamera ever been blackmailed? She couldn't think of a plot where that happened but she'd watched plenty of gangster movies where someone had been, and in those movies, the someone was always shot. But, it might be a good idea to go with Gwen. She'd left Meredith in a real mess, dripping in the toxic goop, wearing Walter's hoodie. She'd ruined her chances at a solo. If she went with Gwen, she could find Meredith and make it up to her somehow.

"Enough time. Shake."

Lindsey shook.

"What are you two girls up to?" Mom looked at them sideways.

"Getting along, like you want us to." Gwen smiled as if she'd eaten the last piece of cheesecake, and put her arm around Lindsey. "Lindsey and I are going to inspect the hotel after the picnic."

"Well, that's wonderful. That's more like it. We're on vacation so we should all get along." Mom hugged them. "Now our picnic."

"Mom!" Jenna yelled. "Watch your nails!"

"Oh, yes, dear." She shook them out in front of her. But Jenna wasn't looking at Mom's nails but at Lindsey and Gwen and their fake sisterly love.

BALLROOMS, BOYS, AND SINGING

Lindsey had to admit the picnic had been fun. They ate their sandwiches, chips, and pop sitting in front of the fake fire, which actually produced enough heat to roast an apple. Well, maybe enough heat to shrivel an already shriveled apple. Lindsey and Gwen had taken off their sweaters and used them as pillows with their feet propped on the couch (not OPPSOOES—OPPSOOES was resigned forever to Ginger).

Jenna and Mom had lain on the couch, Jenna rolling Gwen's cheap bread into balls and popping them into her mouth, while her head rested on Mom's shoulder. They hadn't figured out the T.V. so it still told them that the spa was open 10 a.m. to 10 p.m. daily. Lindsey had seen it on their way to their room. It contained two treadmills and an ab machine, not much of a spa even if it was open late.

"It's nice to see you girls getting along again." Mom said and sighed. "If only you could stay like this, we could change our plans."

Gwen opened a compact and applied a garish pink lipstick. "Want some?" she asked Mom passing her the compact and lipstick.

Mom examined her face in the compact. Lindsey noticed a wrinkle by her mouth that hadn't been there before the announcement. Mom snapped the compact shut and handed it to Gwen. Lindsey could be applying eye shadow too if only she had decided. Decided. Everything hinged on deciding.

"Time to go." Gwen pulled Lindsey to her feet and threw her sweater to her. "Sisters off to see the world." She linked arms with Lindsey.

"Just a sec. I need something." Lindsey snuck into the closet and took Jenna's hippy hat and hid it behind her back. She'd been transformed into a hat thief, but she needed camouflage, from everyone, including herself.

"I want to go! I want to go!" Jenna linked arms with Gwen, who resisted and pushed her off. "We could search for a vending machine. I brought lots of change. We could bring back dessert."

"No, it's only Lindsey and me." Gwen said shoving Lindsey toward the door. "We'll bring you back something."

"Take care of Ginger!" Lindsey mouthed to Jenna while the door slammed. Jenna stood with her head down—sad and abandoned. It ripped at Lindsey's heart. Meredith had looked the same when she'd left the Food Lion. Go, Lindsey. Two outs.

Gwen pulled on Lindsey's arm. "It's this way. And, remember, I don't want anything to do with you unless I need you."

They marched down a hall with flowered flocked wallpaper and burgundy flowered carpeting—no beige in sight. The chandeliers hung low overhead making Lindsey want to duck to avoid them. A sign read *Ballroom* with an arrow to the right.

Gwen stopped and pointed. "I'm going to the Ballroom to meet Marcus and Chris after their choir practice. You can come. I mean if you want."

Lindsey ached to see Chris, but he knew she was the girl who stole his hat. If only she'd given it back. Then she could introduce herself to him and he'd skate with her at the Rink at the Brink. She imagined that the skating rink hung over the Falls and she'd trip over the railing and almost tumble into the surging water, only Chris would catch her in time, lifting her to safety, brushing a curl from his eye as he set her down. But, no, she needed to do the saving.

"No, I'll wander around." She twisted her hair a good twist to get her thinking started.

"Don't go far, in case I need you to prove that I should be here." Gwen sashayed into the Ballroom.

Lindsey smashed Jenna's hat on. She tilted it at an angle so no one could see her eyes and continued down the hall. Rats, she couldn't see. She lifted the rim. Up ahead, a few kids wearing Chinowapi hoodies exited a room. She heard applause and a whoop. She moved closer. A sign by the door read *Crystal Room*. The door opened and she heard singing—a male voice, deep and rich, but not so deep that it was silly, like when Dad serenaded Mom, just deep enough that she shivered in delight. Chris! Of course, Chris would sing like that. Lindsey scooted toward the door and peeked in.

Marcus! Marcus stood on a stage far in the back of the room singing, "O Canada!" The rest of the choir stood behind him on risers. They sang softly, "O Canada, we stand on guard for thee." When they repeated these words, the choir raised their hands and swayed.

Walter, the Hagrid look-alike, stood on a box beside Marcus directing. When the choir raised their voices for "stand on guard for thee," Walter waved his hands like a crazed conductor. He held a baton, which looked tiny as a fairy's in his hand, and dwarfed the kids in the first row. When they finished, the kids whistled and stomped their feet.

"Quiet. Quiet!" Walter waved his arms. "Good as it was, it wasn't good enough. We'll start again." Walter walked over to a thin woman sitting at a battered yellow piano on the edge of the stage. A pony tail sprouted from the top of her head like a cornstalk, and her eyes were green slits.

Walter flipped the pages of her music and pointed. "Begin here, Ms. Norstern."

Ms. Norstern played, her hands bouncing and pouncing up and down the keyboard.

"No, not yet."

She dropped her hands to her side.

He addressed the choir. "Now, sopranos, when you …"

While Walter explained, the kids studied their black books of music and scribbled notes. The same kids who'd run wild at the Food Lion and restaurant now were united in purpose and focused.

"Miss O'Day!" Doctor Schwab came up suddenly behind Lindsey, making her jump. "Doctor Schwab shall be instituting demerits against you for missing choir practice. Afterward, we'll discuss your behavior this afternoon at the Food Lion and walking the halls of the boy's floor, the most disgusting of your multiple misdeeds." She shook her head.

Lindsey whipped around so she was eye-to-eye with Doctor Schwab. "Doctor Schwab, I—"

"Walter!" Doctor Schwab yelled not listening to Lindsey and walking into the Crystal Room. "Walter! I *must* interrupt."

"Again, Schwab?" Walter boomed into the cavernous Crystal Room from the stage. "I know you're new to your job, but you must learn when to interrupt and when to blow your whistle."

"A missing person is here." Doctor Schwab said.

"Our guest soloist?" Walter asked.

Guest soloist! What trouble was she letting herself into now?

"Terrific. Wonderful," he continued. "Welcome. We went ahead without you, with Marcus filling in as soloist."

"Walter," Doctor Schwab said. "She isn't the—"

"Now, Schwab, no need for introductions. We all know our soloist and her famed hats. Yes, yes, know them well from her American Idol appearances."

She'd been on American Idol! Oh, my gosh. Who was she pretending to be? Kelly Clarkson?

"Don't be shy," Walter added. "Please come forward—on stage. We can't see you very well back there, although I'm sure from what I heard of your voice, we could *hear* you."

Lindsey slanted Jenna's hippy hat forward over her eyes and walked toward the stage, passing in between tables draped in purple cloths, Walter's call to sing hypnotizing her. The ballroom smelled of old perfume and alcohol, as if it had hosted hundreds of proms. A prom committee, even with Tamera as the chairperson, would have to do a lot of decorating to make it nice.

As she passed around another table, she realized that she had never sung in public. At school and church she mouthed the words. But she dreamt what it would be like to wear a beautiful gown, glittering jewels, her hair piled high on her head and come out to thundering applause.

She'd bow and the audience would cheer even louder. But when she opened her mouth, they'd boo because they'd realize why she'd been kicked out of third-grade choir.

She forced herself back into the moment—the reality of which was terrible enough, she didn't need to dream one. She twisted her hair into a tight snarl and squeezed her lips until they hurt. She climbed the stairs, dragging her feet like Godzilla treading through a swamp. She blinked from the bright lights on stage and moved toward Marcus, all the choir kids staring down at her from the risers. Marcus mouthed, *"You!"* and gestured to Chris in the back row.

"Marcus," Walter said. "Join the other choir members. You can be our soloist another time." Marcus shoved his way to the second riser of the choir in front of Chris and whispered to him. The other kids whispered and chattered as well, their unity shaken and their focus gone.

"Let me out." Chris said as he pushed forward.

"Choir, please stay where you are." Walter tapped his baton on his stand.

Chris settled back in his spot, muttering.

"You'll all get a chance for an autograph from our soloist. Now, because of the late hour we haven't time for introductions, but if you'd like to warm up, we can accommodate that. What piece you like to warm up with? Ms. Norstern can play most anything."

Ms. Norstern smiled and pounced her hands across the keyboard again, this time, raising them in triumph at the end.

"Thank you, Ms. Norstern."

Ms. Norstern stood and bowed.

"Enough, Ms. Norstern."

Ms. Norstern sat down, her cornstalk pony tail bouncing.

From Lindsey's view on stage, the rest of the room looked dark and evil. Doctor Schwab stood at the bottom of the stairs with her arms crossed, tapping her foot, and waiting for Lindsey (or Lisa). At least up here, she was safe from her. Lindsey remained silent, the sweat popping out on her forehead, her stomach feeling like she had the flu but it was probably the apples.

Walter looked at her. "A warm-up?" he asked.

"Um, now?" Lindsey tucked her hair behind her ear.

"Yes, now." Walter said. "These young people have a curfew and are anxious for their pizza party and skating." The choir cheered.

"Oh, OK." Lindsey twisted her hair. She searched for Meredith. Everyone wore the same hoodie. Meredith's lumberjack shirt should be easy to spot. She could see Marcus and Chris whispering together again. Were they planning something? Certainly not a date with her afterward.

"Now," Walter said.

"Now," Lindsey repeated. But what would a famous singer warm up with? Heck if she knew. She rubbed her forehead, racking her brain through her sources of information: movies and books. Nothing came. Her brain was in a fog. Her heart accelerated to 80 mph. She wondered how many kilometers in Canada that was. Oh, how stupid to think of that now. If she did think of something, she wasn't sure the words would come out from her tight throat.

Chris stepped forward, "Mr. Kleptomanie, you've got to listen." Oh, no, he was going to tell. She'd better say something. She shook out her hands. Think.

"Um, well, high C?" Lindsey squeaked, her voice going up on the C. The choir laughed. Marcus hit Chris on the back. She could make out that he'd said, "She's an idiot." Lindsey twisted her hair until she couldn't and then rewound it.

"Quiet, choir," Walter boomed.

The laughter quieted to a twitter. Lindsey scanned the choir again and found Meredith far in the back behind a tall blonde, almost as though she were hiding.

Walter turned to Lindsey. "High C to start. Well, that really starts things cracking. Maybe something a little lower for the choir."

"Tra, la, la?" Lindsey answered and the choir laughed. "Do, ra, me?" What was she doing? Why was she going along with this? Why was she afraid of Doctor Schwab or Marcus and Chris? Stupid fear always led her into messes. "I'm not—," she began. But wait, she thought of something … yes. That's it. At the idea, her breathing calmed and her heart slowed to 10 mph. She combed out her twisted hair with her fingers. She knew it was right because both Tamera and Annie would do it.

She slanted Jenna's hat and put her hand on her hip. "Excuse me, Walter. I'm not singing alone. Not with these lovely children behind me." She poised her hand. "I'd like to ask one of the lovely young ladies to accompany me. Now, let me see." Lindsey scanned the choir. "That lovely girl in the lumberjack shirt."

Meredith pointed to herself.

"Yes, indeed, come forward, young lady. I believe you and I would make a lovely sound." The words hurried out in such a beautiful flow that they couldn't be hers, but they were. She felt light, inspired, even calm.

Meredith shook her head no.

What was she doing? That wasn't in the plan!

"That chick never sings solo," Marcus called out. "She's chicken."

"Marcus! Stop!" Walter boomed out again. "This is the last interruption I'll take from you. Leave the stage."

"Not fair!" Chris called. "Can't you see—"

"Out both of you." Walter pointed down to Doctor Schwab, who rubbed her hands together. Marcus and Chris hung their heads and shuffled their feet down the stage. Doctor Schwab swept her arm inviting them to sit near her. They continued to a table near the door, whispering to each other.

"Young lady in the shirt, please step forward," Walter said.

"She is ineligible," Doctor Schwab called out.

"Quiet, Schwab!" Walter shouted.

Meredith stepped forward, and then stepped back. Why wasn't she taking her chance? Then, Lindsey knew why. Why she was hidden behind the tall blonde in the choir, why she'd given up Ginger, and why she asked her to save her from Doctor Schwab.

"Oh, she's shy," Lindsey said to herself. "Excuse me," she said out loud to the tall blonde and pulled Meredith to the center of the stage. Meredith stumbled forward. "I thought this was what you wanted, Meredith?" she asked.

Meredith stared at her with wide eyes and nodded.

"Then come on. We'll do it together. I won't leave you this time."

"What would you like to sing?" Walter asked.

Lindsey nudged Meredith and she whispered, "Silent Night."

"Silent Night," Lindsey called to Walter. "We'll sing Silent Night."

"Good selection. Choir, take out Silent Night. Ms. Norstern, please." Walter raised his hands and Ms. Norstern played an introduction. After the introduction, silence. Neither Lindsey nor Meredith nor the choir sang.

"Shall we begin again?" Walter asked.

"You can do it, Meredith." Lindsey put her arm around Meredith. "I believe in you." Then she said to Walter, "Yes, Walter, please start again."

Walter nodded to Ms. Norstern, who began again. Meredith opened her mouth. Lindsey stared into it, daring a note to come out. She waved her hands like a magician, Abracadabra. Please, Meredith.

"Si—" Meredith sang.

"That's it, Meredith," Lindsey encouraged her. "Louder."

"Silent night, holy night." Meredith's sang out.

"Yes," Lindsey called. "Beautiful."

Meredith smiled and sang even louder and with more feeling. She drifted away from herself and into the music, lost in the beautiful words and sounds. The choir echoed behind her, swaying back and forth. The awkward, paranoid Meredith vanished, and in her place glowed a sparkling singer—a princess in a Disney movie. Lindsey shivered when Meredith sang, "Sleep in heavenly peace." Reaching so high to pierce the heavens on the word *peace*.

When she finished, the kids whistled and stomped.

"Well, my Lumberjack girl." Walter wiped a tear away. "Why have you hidden this talent? With you, we didn't need a guest soloist."

Meredith beamed.

"Darlings, darlings! I'm sorry to be late. I saw a rat at the store and had to see justice done. But now I'm here to practice with you lovely children for tomorrow night. You did wait for me, didn't you? I *am* your soloist, Lydia!"

From around the tables, the real soloist, the woman from the Food Lion appeared. Lindsey and Meredith laughed in delight. The Rat lady was the soloist!

"Wonderful, wonderful," Walter was saying. "We have so many soloists."

"But you only need one," Lydia sang out and then coughed and cleared her throat. "Oh, my, I need a warm-up to sing so high. I may have yelled a bit today."

In the commotion of the Lydia's arrival, Lindsey decided to escape. "Goodbye, Meredith!" Lindsey hugged her. "You were wonderful. And, you got your chance at a solo." Lindsey ran down the steps of the stage and out the door.

She hurried to the Ballroom where she found Gwen snatching a pepperoni from a pizza box. When Lindsey came in, she dropped the lid. Then she reopened it. "Have some, Lindsey."

"Come on, Gwen. Let's go. You know this is wrong."

"I know no such thing. Besides, since when are you making decisions? Haven't you pretended to be somebody else all day?"

"I'm making the decisions because you don't seem to know right from wrong. We need to be with Mom and Jenna. I'm leaving even if you're not. I'm going back to our room where we belong and be who we are. Now come on."

"Miss O'Day!" Doctor Schwab called. "Miss O'Day!"

"Now, Gwen!" Lindsey placed her hands on her hips. "We're leaving now."

"No, I'm staying," Gwen said.

Doctor Schwab marched in. "Miss—"

"I'll never forgive you, Lindsey," Gwen said and ran off with her.

When they arrived back at their room, Lindsey pounded on the door.

"I'm not letting you in," someone inside called. "Unless you bought me something from the vending machine."

IT'S ONLY MAKE BELIEVE

The next morning, Lindsey, her sisters, and Mom, two by two, climbed down the hill to the wax museum, passing the square box hotels and souvenir shops and toward the better part of town with the Falls and attractions. Lindsey felt Ginger wiggle underneath her coat, and she swung Meredith's bag by her side, filled with water bottles for Ginger and food. A shot of sunshine warmed her face and cool mist sprinkled her. Lindsey smiled in anticipation. The Falls!

But no trees or nature filled the street and lead them to the Falls. Only dark, gothic haunted houses, bright red and yellow video game arcades, 3D movie palaces with cutouts of the shows (3D dinosaurs or SpongeBob), and glow-in-the dark golf courses in purple and black. A natural wonder may lurk somewhere but everything Lindsey saw was human-made—loud, noisy, tacky, and wonderful! A Carnival!

Each building called to them: *"See SpongeBob in 3D," "Step closer but watch out for the guill-o-tine."* Far in the distance, a tall green glass hotel and a skinny tower with the words *Niagara Casino* rose above it all.

In her excitement, Lindsey grabbed Jenna's hand but Jenna pulled away. Her hippy hat whipped off down the hill, spinning past the giant plastic gorilla perched on top of a building and landed in front of a haunted house.

"My hat! You made me lose my hat!" Jenna yelled. "I knew you didn't want to be my sister." She chased after it—an unstoppable force careening downhill on wobbly heels. She skidded to a stop in front of a wooden chest tied in chains with a sign that read *Keep Hands Clear!* The chest rattled and spoke, *"Don't get bit!"* Jenna screamed. She shoved her hat on so her ears stuck out from her skinny hair, and tottered back to them.

"That horrible box talked to me!" She yanked on Mom's arm. "Someone's inside and they're dying!" She scanned like a wild thing from Gwen to Mom to Lindsey,

"Oh, Jenna, honey. It's pretend." Mom patted Jenna's back. "Calm down."

Gwen crossed her arms across her chest, a grumpy, older Jenna. "Don't be hysterical. You knew that when you looked all this up."

"Give me Ginger!" Jenna yelled to Lindsey.

"Shh!" Lindsey covered Jenna's mouth. "Mom's here."

Jenna shoved her hand down. "I need something to love that's not going away. Give her to me. It'll make me feel better."

"No, I can't trust you with her. Here, have her bag." Lindsey thrust the sequined bag at her.

"What are you girls talking about?" Mom asked. "Ginger candy? And where did you get that bag?"

"Well, um ..." Lindsey spied statues of British guards standing at attention outside a one-story, brown brick building packed between two brightly lit video arcades. Above its arched wooden doors, a sign read, *"François Trippard's Wax Museum. Are they real? See if you can tell."*

"Jenna!" Lindsey called. "We're here! We're here! It's your Meateaters." Lindsey knew the guards were Beefeaters, with their red-striped knickers and berets, but Jenna had called them Meateaters when they had read about them on Wikipedia and they'd laughed and laughed. Lindsey felt a flash of sadness. She wanted the old days back when Jenna loved her and Mom wasn't, well, what she was.

"Tacky," said Gwen. "This museum is supremely obsolete. Look, we're the only ones headed here; all the people are headed to Ripley's Believe it or Not. If I yelled there'd be an echo."

Jenna opened her mouth to yell but Gwen clamped it shut. "They're probably at the new ice skating rink, too, The Rink at the Brink." She then hissed at Lindsey, "And, we could have been too if you'd let us pretend to be choir members." At that, a crowd of kids all wearing dark clothes stormed into the video arcade next door.

"You are exactly correct, Gwendolyn." Jenna sniffed and pushed her hat further on her head. "Lindsey's enthusiasm is extremely illogical. This place is fantastically tacky."

"Oh, girls. You're at it again," Mom said as she led the way into the dark lobby with purple carpeting and black walls toward the ticket window. Wax figures circled the room, entombed in glass cases: Frankenstein and his wife; wolf man and his; and Dracula, all alone—no wife for him. A woman sat behind a ticket window, her lips smeared with blood red lipstick as if she'd kissed Dracula right after his lunch. Maybe *she* was his wife! Lindsey giggled. She began to whisper the joke to Jenna, but Jenna stood in front of Frankenstein, who was tall enough to be a basketball player.

"My mom's to be electrified like you, Frank." Jenna stared up into his dead eyes.

"No, I'm not, Jenna," Mom said, passing out tickets. "I'm going to be radiated, which shrinks the cancer. Now let's have fun. No more morbid thoughts."

"Morbid, zorbid, I hate morbid," Jenna jumped and waved her hands in front of Frankenstein. "Blink! He doesn't blink!"

Gwen pulled her down. "It's a good thing no one's here. She's gone nuts. Make her stop."

"She's not nuts, Gwen," Lindsey said. "She's sad."

"Yeah, I'm sad," Jenna said. "Because of you two. Where'd you go last night? Leaving me behind. And, taking *my* hat." Jenna clenched Meredith's sequined bag tighter. "You take my hat, I take Ginger. Give me Ginger."

Mom sank onto a bench next to Frankenstein with her head in her hands.

"Look what you've done." Gwen sat next to Mom and hugged her.

Jenna cried as if she'd run over a puppy. "Mommy, Mommy, are you sick?"

"No, I'm fine, Jenna." Mom shook her head and her curls moved as if waggling their disapproval at the girls too. "It's the bickering that I can't stand."

Jenna's craziness just wouldn't do. "Come on, Jenna." Lindsey tugged Jenna toward the first room of wax figures. "Let's see what they've got. It's why we're here."

Jenna yanked her arm away and stuck her nose in the air. "If you want me to go, give me Ginger."

"Your coat doesn't have room." Lindsey said in a whisper. Jenna's short blue coat reached only to her waist.

"I can carry her in Meredith's bag."

"What is this Ginger you keep talking about?" Mom asked getting up from the bench. "Let me see it. Did Aunt Kelly give you ginger candy? I can't believe you'd like it enough to fight over."

Before Jenna could say, Gwen shoved Jenna from behind, pushing her into the next room, and Mom followed.

"Oh!" Jenna's shoulders drooped and she staggered on her heels. "It's educational!" Wax figures filled the room recreating historical scenes. "Abraham Lincoln, George Washington." She pouted her lower lip." Yuck. We should ask for our money back. Where are the celebrities? I demand celebrities."

The girls and Mom wandered the room. Jenna and Mom stopped in front of a scene with a sick person in bed and their family sitting around them. On a bench nearby, an elderly couple sat looking at the figures. They wore matching blue flowered shirts and their gray hair was cut short—an identical husband and wife.

"My mom is retched sick, too," Jenna said to the couple.

"Oh, my." The woman stroked Jenna's hair. "We're sorry to hear that."

The man took out a yellow pack of gum from his pocket. "Have a stick of Fruity Fruits."

Jenna shook her head. The woman fumbled in her purse, and held a peppermint candy.

"Want a peppermint?" The woman offered Jenna the roll. "The whole roll?"

"No, thank you." Jenna shook her head.

Wow, Jenna had said no to someone offering her something. Doctor Schwab wouldn't know her today. Jenna walked away from the couple and deliberately bumped into Mom. Then, she squeezed Mom so hard she almost knocked her over again.

"Whoa, Jenna, honey," Mom said holding her back.

"Maybe that person has what you have, Mom. Frankenstein can electrolyze you all."

"Oh, Jenna, please be happy." Mom hugged Jenna back. "This is what you've been waiting for. I don't feel sick now. Enjoy the museum." She arranged Jenna's hair into a straight arrow behind her back. "Lindsey, please take her and have some fun."

"Come on, Jenna." Lindsey took Jenna's hand. "I'll find you some celebrities." Gwen stepped in and pushed Lindsey's hand down.

"No need for that." Gwen wrapped her arm around Jenna. "I'll entertain her. I had world history this year."

"But Jenna wants—"

"But I know what Jenna *needs*."

"Boy, I'm getting tired of this," Lindsey said to Ginger and then looked up to see her mother staring at her. She smiled. Her mother didn't smile back.

"Follow me, all." Gwen kept Jenna's hand in her two. "I shall elucidate."

Lindsey plugged her ears. She'd had enough of Gwen. Last night she'd done the right thing. She'd made Gwen come back and now she knew that celebrities were the right thing. No doubts. Gwen couldn't be worse than Dr. Schwab, although Lindsey had to admit that she'd run away from Doctor Schwab last night like always. Why did she always run away? After all, a person couldn't get expelled from a school that person didn't attend, and it couldn't go on that person's real high school record, could it?

"Do you know, Ginger, sweet doggie?" Lindsey asked, and then answered for Ginger: "Don't be stupid, Lindsey. You're acting like Meredith—par-a-noid."

Lindsey wandered the room: Abraham Lincoln, Franklin Roosevelt. Boring. Lindsey wanted the celebrities as badly as Jenna. And, Gwen did too if she'd admit it. Finally, they were on the last scene in the room. Oh, no, a recreation of the French Revolution, with Marie Antoinette, draped in sparkling diamond jewels and purple and gold finery, kneeling headless next to the guillotine. Gwen had written a twelve-page paper about the French Revolution even though only six were required. She could go on and on all day! Maybe Lindsey could sneak out. To her left an exit sign pointed down a hallway. But before she could, Jenna screamed. She'd seen the wax figure of Marie Antoinette without her head, and held her own head in Mom's arms.

"This wax museum is terrible," she cried. "I want to go home. I want Daddy. I want Ginger."

Lindsey couldn't stand it. Poor Jenna was a mess. She dashed to the exit.

A second later, she rushed back. "Jenna, Jenna, it's not an exit. It's another room." She pulled on Jenna's arm. "Another good room."

"Stop it," Gwen said. "You're acting like a lunatic. Someone will see you. Besides I'm taking care of Jenna." Forget that. Gwen's power over her ceased. Lindsey stood a little taller. Jenna needed to be brought back.

"Jenna, it's movie stars." Lindsey jumped up and down in determination. "Like on the Classic Films channel! But they're not in black and white—they're in color. There's Marilyn Monroe, Cary Grant! Both the happy and sad Judy Garland. Come on, Jenna." Lindsey flapped her free hand.

"Go on, Jenna." Mom pushed Jenna toward Lindsey. "Have fun. I'll just sit out here." She sat down on the bench near the wax figures that recreated the sick scene.

Lindsey and Jenna rushed to the next room, where movie stars from all the eras, old time ones, like Katherine Hepburn, stood next to black clunky phones, and new time ones, like Reese Witherspoon, held a hot pink cell phones and fluffy white dogs. Jenna twirled in the center, her face shining.

"See, Jenna. I told you it was great." Lindsey danced around her.

Gwen walked to the statue of Marilyn Monroe.

"I'm as gorgeous as Marilyn!" Gwen sauntered up and down the room, swinging her hips.

"You really put your hips into!" Jenna laughed. "Some like it hot!"

"Wait! Let me take your picture!" Lindsey dug in her pocket for her camera, holding on to Ginger with the other. "Sorry, Ginger. I need to put you down." Lindsey sat Ginger in a dusty corner behind Clark Gable as Rhett Butler in *Gone with the Wind.* Ginger's head peeped out of Chris' hat and she watched the girls. With both her hands free, Lindsey was ready for fun. "Pose, Jenna!"

"Look at me. I'm Marilyn too." Jenna stuck her rear out and walked around making little steps on her strappy shoes. She laughed so hard she bent over.

Lindsey rushed to the other side of the room, "Take a picture of me with Bette Davis!" Jenna took the camera and snapped away. "Oh, dawlings," Lindsey pretended to suck on a cigarette. She coughed. "How *are* you?"

What fun! Her soul lost a few pounds and swung higher, lighter, and freer. If only Mom could see them, she'd know they *could* get along. Mom appeared by the door smiling and waved. She'd seen!

"Lindsey!" Jenna yelled. "It's the best! It's Elizabeth Taylor with a dog just like ours!" Lindsey glanced over to see if Mom had noticed Jenna's comment, but Mom was still smiling. She probably thought they were pretending.

"Lindsey, look! The lady who went over the Falls in the barrel." Jenna ran over to Lindsey and kissed her. "You're the best to know about this museum." Could life get any better?

"Hey, it's the chick who stole my hat." Lindsey jumped. Chris stood in the doorway of the room with Marcus behind. Oh, my gosh, look at him! He wore a green sweater, with a gold and brown bird embroidered in the center and over it he wore a blue wool letter jacket with the number 12 sewn on the sleeve in brilliant yellow. No hoodie for the hottie. Then she remembered what she'd been doing and the fun drained out of her. Had he seen her dancing around, like a, like a, Jenna?

"She's the same girl who pretended to be our soloist," Marcus called.

"So, girl," Chris continued. "Could you please give me back my hat? We sing by the Falls tonight, and I'd like it. You know, to keep me warm."

If he only knew that his hat was in a dusty corner stuffed to the brim with a fat dog. But if she didn't say anything, how would he know? He could have lost it after all.

"You mean this?" Jenna held his hat high like a trophy with Ginger hidden inside.

"Hey!" Chris yelled. "What did you do to it? It's all fat."

"What is going on here, Lindsey?" Mom stood behind her. "Who are these boys and why are they saying you stole something? Answers, please, young lady."

Just then Chris noticed Gwen. "Hey, you're the girl from the Food Lion. You were supposed to meet us last night. You never said you knew the girl who stole my hat. Why didn't you get it back for me?"

"But, Chris, I, just, it's just a hat," Gwen stuttered, moving toward Marcus.

"Just a hat? It's *my* hat. So do I get my hat back or what?" Chris held his hands open. "These chicks are nuts." Marcus nodded his head.

"Just try and get it." Jenna rushed out the side door of the wax museum marked "*Exit Emergency Use Only*," moving fast despite her wobbly shoes. The alarm sounded—*Weeoo weeoo*!

"Jenna! What are you doing?" Lindsey started to run after her but stopped. Gwen stood and smiled at Marcus.

"Gwen, are you helping or what?"

"You're right." She stepped away from Marcus. "What do you want me to do?"

"Explain everything to Mom, and I'll get Jenna."

At that, Mom collapsed onto a bench with a wax figure of President Obama sitting on it. "Just tell me what this Ginger is ..."

FINDING MORE THAN EXPECTED

Lindsey opened the door of the wax museum that led to Clifton Hill, setting off the alarm again, and raced outside after Jenna. She snaked her way into the middle of another typical Niagara Falls crowd full of thick coats, baby strollers, and yelling and laughing families.

"Ow!" she hopped on one foot. Someone had stepped on her toe!

She scooted to the front of the crowd, just behind a couple wearing yellow and blue University of Michigan coats and hats. She peered around them. A red hat bounced in the crowd about a block ahead of her and crossed the street. At least Jenna's hippy hat made good identification. But, oh, please, God, keep her safe. No more karma, only praying—and action.

The light turned red, halting Lindsey. Jenna's hippy hat still traveled ahead with the crowd across the street. What if Jenna tripped or lost her hat again? She could be killed the crazy way she was acting.

Sweat formed on her forehead and other unmentionable spots. She tried to calm herself by breathing deeply (in, out). She stomped her feet and rubbed her hands together in frustration. Jenna's hat moved ahead another block, further and further up Clifton Hill, and away from her.

A crowd of kids her own age formed around her, bumping and shoving her in the back. They wore dark hoodies. Wait a minute. She leaned to look at one of the hoodies: Chinowapi High Choir. Oh, no! Not Walter and Doctor Schwab! They must have left the wax museum at the same time.

Lindsey heard one of the girls in the crowd ask, "Where do we go next?"

"The lame SkyWheel," a boy answered.

The SkyWheel! Lindsey smacked her head. Of course. That was Jenna's destination.

The light turned green, and Lindsey sped across the street and down the block.

"Excuse me," she said and pushed her way through a cluster of people. "Pardon me," she said and sped around another cluster and past a single person. "Excuse me … Pardon me."

She made good progress too, closing in on the bouncing red hat in the crowd up ahead, with only one block between her and it. Now it crossed the street again. Lindsey ran after it, but the traffic light flashed a warning countdown: 5, 4, 3, 2, 1. Stopped!

Lindsey collapsed with her hands on her knees catching her breathe. The chrysanthemum of a SkyWheel with its water droplet gondolas loomed in front of her, perched between a Jim Thorton's and a Pizza Plaza. Jenna would be almost to the SkyWheel ticket booth by now. Lindsey imagined Jenna begging for a ticket or inventing a story of why she had no parents. Lindsey had to stop her. But how? She jumped up to see over the crowd to watch Jenna's hat.

Suddenly, a gust of wind tossed the hat into the air and sent it bouncing between the families bustling to the SkyWheel. Jenna sped after it. A man in a dark coat swooped to pick it up. She smiled at him and began chattering, gesturing with her hands like in a silent film, which Jenna hated watching. That was it. She couldn't wait for the light. This stranger might not just be offering her peppermint.

She ran into the street, holding her hand like a traffic cop. She wove between the cars that snaked bumper-to-bumper down Clifton Hill, playing a pedestrian in a video game.

Drivers beeped and yelled, "Hey, what're you doing? Are you nuts? You'll get killed."

"Emergency," she yelled back not even taking the time to say excuse me. Exhaust fumes stung her ankles. She steadied her hand on the hood of a black car to maneuver around it and onto the sidewalk.

She took a deep breath as she reached it, safe with only burnt ankles to show for the risk. Now, where was Jenna? Still in the same spot, talking to the man over by Jim Thorton's. Lindsey zigzagged between the families, and grabbed Jenna's hat from the man.

"Thank you," Lindsey said. "I'm her sister. I'll take care of her."

The man smiled, tucked his head down, and walked away. Pride swelled up in her. It must be how Superman felt. She'd saved Jenna from true danger. Lindsey offered the hat to Jenna.

"Jenna, you're not supposed to talk to—"

Jenna's mouth opened and her eyebrows flew up for a brief moment. Then, they both thrust down into a deep, angry scowl.

"He was giving me back my hat." Jenna smashed it on with her free hand. Ginger sat perched on her other arm, her tail hanging down.

Lindsey took Meredith's bag and adjusted Jenna's hat. "Jenna, why did you run away?"

"I'm not talking to you." Jenna walked around Lindsey but Lindsey stuck out her foot to block her. Jenna walked the other way but Lindsey ran around and stood in her way. Jenna spun and ran forward, but not fast enough for Lindsey—flip flops win over high heels every time.

"We're trying to get in the store here, girls." A family with a baby stroller complained behind them. Lindsey and Jenna scrambled out of their way. As the door to Jim Thorton's opened, Lindsey smelled the coffee and warmth but she dragged Jenna over to the side of the Pizza Palace, out of the crowd and the wind.

"Jenna. Tell me what you're up to." Lindsey shook her hands. "Please."

Tears formed in Jenna's eyes. Lindsey noticed for the first time the dark circles under them.

"I want to be with Ginger." Jenna kissed Ginger. "She's mine. We're going to ride the SkyWheel together."

"But, Jenna." Lindsey touched her shoulder. "We've got to give her *and* the hat back."

"No, I'm not losing Ginger." Jenna hugged Ginger tight. Ginger squealed like a pampered pig. "I'm already losing everything. My mom, my sisters. I won't lose Ginger too. There is only so much a girl can take." Jenna tossed her black hair back and her hat fell off again.

Lindsey laughed, but then picked up the hat and placed it gently on Jenna's head. She combed Jenna's hair back into an arrow down her back, but it didn't reset her. Her dark eyes still burned at Lindsey and she shook from the chilled wind.

"I understand." Lindsey hugged her. "I'll take you."

"Yeah, right." Jenna bounced poor Ginger higher in her arms. "You'll change your mind. You'll say it's too expensive. You'll say we have to save the money for something else. You'll say—"

"OK, OK. I get it." Lindsey held up her hand. "But this time I'll really take you. Aunt Angie would agree that you're a very important person to spend her money on. Give me Ginger so I can hide her, and you can concentrate on walking in those shoes and keeping your hat on."

A long silver fence marked the entrance to the SkyWheel. They lined up behind high schoolers and families, waiting in jumbled bunches. The wind whipped around them. It would be a long wait. Already she could see the sun tilting behind Clifton Hill. How worried would Mom be? On top of that, Lindsey had never paid for a ride before or rode without Mom or Dad.

"See how tall it is." Jenna strained her neck to look at the top of the SkyWheel. "It must be 5,000 million miles up. Ouch, my neck hurts from looking." She rubbed the back of it.

Lindsey gulped as she gazed at the glass bubble gondolas that had looked like water droplets from far away, spinning around the SkyWheel. They would ride in those? Sweat beads formed on her forehead. Ginger whined inside her coat.

"It's OK, Ginger." She said in a whisper to her coat. "We're only going up as high as the Statue of Liberty." But that was pretty high! Lindsey steeled herself. Annie, after all, had gone down the Falls, which really was 5,000 million miles down, give or take 4,999 million miles.

These were just glass bubbles going around and around, and not falling. She hoped.

"Give me the money." Jenna held out her hand. "I'll buy the tickets. You're too chicken."

Lindsey shook her head. "No, I'll do it. I promise. I'm not changing my mind."

Jenna ran to the front of the line and back again counting the number of people in front of them.

"Only six more!" she sang out.

She ran back to the front and came back again.

"Four more!" She began to run ahead again but Lindsey held out her arm.

"Stop. I get it. It's almost our turn."

Jenna stood still as a statue. Lindsey had to push her forward when it's their turn.

"How many, please?" the ticket agent asked, a girl about Gwen's age with orange glasses and a tattoo on her arm. Lindsey studied it—either a winged dinosaur or a chicken. She couldn't decide.

"How many?" the ticket agent asked again.

Lindsey read the prices. "Two, please. One adult and one child." She gulped.

"That'll be sixteen loonies." The ticket agent frowned at Lindsey and pushed her orange glasses higher on her nose.

Loonies? What are loonies? She never heard of that. Canadians used dollars. She looked at Jenna. Jenna shrugged.

"You're holding up the line. Others are waiting to get on. Sixteen loonies." The ticket agent said it as bossy as Gwen would if she were handing out tickets.

"I'm sorry," Jenna said. "But we only have money. Our mom is dying and we want to go on this ride." The tears welled in Jenna's eyes again. "Do something Lindsey. I have to ride!'

"Um, well." Lindsey stuttered. What should she do? "Maybe we'll come back—with the loonies." Lindsey backed away, knocking into the family behind them.

"Lindsey!" Jenna called. "Aren't you going to do something? I want to ride with Ginger!"

"Jenna, I don't have loonies." Lindsey thought for a moment. "But I do have you. I could barter one loonie sister for a ride on the SkyWheel." She surprised herself at being able to find something funny when she felt ready to have a heart attack.

The ticket agent laughed. "That's a good one." She smiled and pushed her glasses up. "Relax, kid. Loonies *are* Canadian money. I do that to all the Americans but you're the first with a good joke. If you don't have loonies, it's 18.32 American."

"Oh, wow." Lindsey glanced at Jenna who scowled at her. "I mean, thanks. That's not overpriced at all." Lindsey handed her one of Aunt Angie's crisp $20 bills, grabbed the change, and headed through the gates toward their glass bubbles, the doors of which slid open and away like the wings of a bird.

"I'm not scared anymore, Lindsey." Jenna jumped into the gondola.

"Don't swing it, Jenna!" Lindsey stood back, holding tight to her Ginger bundle.

"It doesn't swing, Linds." Jenna jiggled back and forth but the gondola held steady.

Lindsey stepped forward, putting her foot in.

"Oh, my," someone behind her called. "Is that little girl pregnant?"

Startled, Lindsey fell onto the hard bench inside the gondola. She unbuttoned her coat and Ginger's head popped out, like she'd given birth to a mutant. The gondola was warm and quiet, insulated from the wind and people. It smelled like a new plastic toy. The doors slid closed, locking them in. Outside, she could see the wide white metal legs that supported the SkyWheel and the spokes of its wheel with its million metal crisscrosses.

"Look, Lindsey." Jenna walked up and down in the gondola. "It's as big as an elevator. I'll sit across from you on the other bench so we can watch each other scream." Jenna sat on the bench and searched around. Four buttons dotted the ceiling of the gondola: a red emergency, a green mute, a white light, and a green for fan.

"Do we push a button to make it move?" She held her finger over the red emergency button.

"No, Jenna. Don't touch them. What if you called someone and they saw our dog? It's just because people are still getting on. You know, like a Ferris Wheel."

The car jolted upward. "Oh, now, we're going." Jenna gazed. "It's tickling my stomach."

An announcer came on the speaker overhead. "Welcome to the Niagara SkyWheel. For your safety, do not lean against the gondola doors. The SkyWheel rises to   5 feet."

"Thank you, Mr. Announcer." The SkyWheel jolted to a stop. Jenna fell back. The SkyWheel started up and she fell forward.

"I'm scared here alone I'm coming over." Jenna walked across the bubble and cuddled next to Lindsey. "You're the greatest, Lindsey."

This was terrific, Lindsey decided. She should lean back and enjoy it. Hadn't she rescued Jenna and got them on without loonies? Wasn't she going *up* in a bubble like Annie had gone *down* in a barrel? Gwen couldn't say that it was tacky, no, it was thrilling.

"Lindsey, look below."

Her stomach tingled at the thought of looking down but she snuck a peek. "Everything is cement!" Below them spread the plaza and the rooftops of the flat buildings: Jim Thorton's, Pizza Place, the arcades.

"Hi, SpongeBob," Jenna called and waved as they passed the cut-out of SpongeBob perched on top of the 3D movie house.

"See how tiny that family is who wanted us to move." Jenna pointed a finger to the father with the stroller directly below them. "I can squish them with my fingers." And, from up this high, it did look like Jenna had the man with the stroller between her fingers and squished him. "Smush, smush, smush!"

"Look, Jenna, there's the Falls. Both of them. I can see the Falls!" Out in the distance beyond the cement rose Niagara Falls: the straight American Falls and then further to the right hidden by a cloud of mist, the Canadian Horseshoe Falls. The rocks below the American Falls shone rough and jagged.

Before she could take everything in, Ginger struggled and pushed against her, digging her nails into her chest. Ow—sharp little knives. Lindsey pulled Ginger from Chris' hat. Her pink bow and tongue hung down, quivering. Her entire body convulsed, her stomach heaved, like she needed to throw up. Had she suffocated her?

Jenna burst out, "Lindsey! Something's horribly, awfully wrong with Ginger!"

SEARCHING FOR ANSWERS

Something was!

"Jenna, take my coat off of me and put it on the floor. I'll put her down."

Jenna pulled Lindsey's coat off, and Lindsey placed Ginger on her it between the benches. Ginger rooted and circled before lying down, panting and whining. She stretched her belly so she was twice as long—almost as long as a submarine sandwich. Meredith had kept saying she had something to tell her. Was this it? That Ginger was sick? Would Lindsey have to take Ginger back to Meredith at the hotel and say, "I'm sorry, Meredith. Here's your dog. She was OK until the SkyWheel." Lindsey would hand Ginger to Meredith, and Ginger's head would droop and her tongue loll, with those horrible XX's in her eyes. Nothing Tamera or anyone had everyone done.

No, she wasn't letting that happen. Lindsey shook herself into action. If she could help Meredith and Jenna, she could help Ginger. She pressed the mute button overhead to stop the announcer so she could concentrate. The announcer had been droning on, "150,000 U.S. gallons of water splash over the Falls each second..." She pushed her hair behind her ear, and twisted.

"Look in Meredith's bag, Jenna. Maybe there's medicine." Lindsey sat back on her heels. "Like in that old movie where they give the man the nitroglycerin and it saves his life at the last moment."

"Yeah, I remember that movie." Jenna put her hands on her cheeks. "And, if the man jiggled the nitroglycerin before swallowing it would blow everyone up. That was a good movie. I cried and cried. But I also liked the one where the bad guy wouldn't give the dying man the medicine. And the dying man begged and begged and still the bad guy wouldn't—"

"Jenna!" Lindsey glared at her.

"OK, OK. Let's see." Jenna dug into the bag and pulled out a small white package wrapped in cellophane. "Doggie mints! Cool." Then she dug back in. "Comb, a brush." Jenna held the brush so Lindsey could see. "That's the sweetest brush I ever saw. So tiny and gold with little pictures of dogs."

"Jenna, get serious. Ginger is in trouble."

Jenna frowned and burrowed back into the bag. "Got something this time. A water bottle." Jenna held up a silver water bottle with a poodle etched in it. "Meredith has the coolest stuff."

"Quick, let me have it!" Lindsey grabbed it and splashed water on her hand. Ginger licked it but she still panted and twitched like a broken wind-up toy. Oh, if she could only figure out what was wrong.

"It didn't help. Nothing will help. She has cancer," Jenna cried. "She's going to die! Everybody's going to die!" Jenna dropped the bag and stomped to the window. "Everyone's going to die," She mumbled.

"No, they aren't. Let me think."

Jenna sat back down, putting her hands through her hair so it stood up like antennas. "Are you thinking Lindsey? Twist your hair, it always helps."

The SkyWheel stopped.

"Oh, great! Now, we're stuck!" Jenna called. They were back on top with the cement and the Barbie-sized people below.

"I don't see the family to squish anymore." Jenna looked back at Lindsey. "By the way, what did that one lady say to you?"

"You mean the lady when we got on? Oh, she said … Jenna, look at Ginger now!" Ginger had stood back up, and now she paced back and forth. She stopped and her whole body convulsed. "Do you think it's the green goop? Her body could be convulsing to get rid of it."

"Yeah, the green goop." Jenna nodded her head. Then, she shook it. "Wouldn't she have done that last night, and wouldn't she be throwing up or, you know, something brown coming out the other end?"

Lindsey rubbed her forehead. What makes a dog do this? Pant and squirm and be so *fat*. "Doesn't a dog foam at the mouth when it has rabies, Jenna?"

"Yeah, like in the movie where the dog charges the boy. Yes. But I wouldn't say that is foam, would you?" Jenna knelt beside Ginger who snarled at her. She startled back into the gondola door. "Oh, no, I touched the door. I'm not supposed to touch the door! Should I press the Emergency button?"

"Don't touch any of those buttons, Jenna." Her eyes turned into slits. She continued puzzling it out. "No, there's no foam. What other sickness do dogs get? What movies have we seen with sick dogs?" Lindsey covered her face with her hands. She peeked between her fingers at Jenna. "Remember that one movie where the horse was sick and convulsing and he laid down and horses aren't supposed to lie down."

"Yeah, but that horse wasn't sick—" They stared at each other and then said together, "Pregnant!"

"And, that's what the lady said to me when I got on, Jenna. Duh, Ginger's having puppies, Jenna. She's not dying. She's having babies."

"Ahh!" Jenna screamed. "Aren't we supposed to boil water?"

"Poor Ginger." Lindsey reached down to touch her belly. Now that she looked close, she could see the form of the puppies squirming inside. Ginger growled. Lindsey and Jenna jumped back. They clung to each other.

"Lindsey!" Jenna looked at Lindsey. "I'm scared. I don't want the puppies to die!"

"The ride'll be over soon, and then we'll take her to the vet or something." Lindsey gave herself a pep talk: I've got to stay in charge. No doubts. The gondola slowed and stopped again, suspending them out over the Falls. Their gondola inched down a little further when people below got off and others got on. Finally, their gondola stopped at the bottom and the doors flew open.

Lindsey lifted Ginger but she squirmed and snarled at her and scurried under the bench, like an angry old man on his porch. Lindsey put her arm out to block Jenna. "Don't get off," she ordered. "I can't pick up Ginger. I don't know what to do."

"Lindsey, you said you were thinking of something. That you were going to *save* her. You should have twisted your hair."

"I *am*. But even if I *could* pick her up, we can't carry her twitching like this—she'd fall out of my arms. We'll ask a guard, attendant, whatever they're called." Lindsey looked behind them for an attendant. She only saw tons of kids crowding to get on the SkyWheel. She saw a kid with pointy hair—Marcus! It was the group from the choir. Meredith would be with them! Lindsey scanned the crowd. Instead of standing off by herself, Meredith chatted with Chris and Marcus. Chris! Everybody had a crush on him.

Lindsey stepped out of the gondola.

"Meredith! Meredith!" she called. She saw the SkyWheel attendant coming toward her, with a furious look on his face. He yelled and waved to them to get off. Yikes, they were in trouble. She rushed back in.

"She can't hear me again. Jenna, you yell."

Jenna stepped out.

"Meredith! Meredith! You-who Meredith."

Lindsey saw Meredith search around for who was calling and then go back to laughing at something Marcus said. Jenna screamed as loud as she could and waved her hands. Lindsey put her hands over her ears—Jenna had strong lungs. "Mer-e-dith!"

This time Marcus pointed out Jenna to Meredith. Meredith recognized them and rushed past the attendant and the people waiting. When she stepped in, her panting matched Ginger's.

"Meredith, it's Ginger," Lindsey said. "She won't let us touch her. Is she having puppies? Is that what you should have told me?"

Meredith crawled under the bench. "Gin-Gin, it's your mommy," Meredith murmured, soothing Ginger and gathering her up, Lindsey's coat and all. "Sorry, Lisa. I should have told you."

Lindsey shivered and said, "No problem."

Out of the corner of her eye, Lindsey noticed the attendant coming closer. "Let's get out of here before that attendant puts us in jail. We should go somewhere quiet where she can have the puppies." But where? Her stomach churned. Oh, she hated this, but it was up to her. Meredith and Jenna and Ginger and Gwen and Mom—*Everyone!* counted on her to do the right thing. "Come on."

"Young ladies, you have to leave the—" The attendant had his stick out.

"We are, Mr., don't put us in jail," Jenna yelled as she hobbled out of the gondola and smack into Doctor Schwab.

"Oh, hi, Wilma," Jenna said.

"Miss Jenna, we meet again. I hope your mother enjoyed the gift. I see you are still wearing those unfortunate shoes."

"I gave my other shoes to my mother. She doesn't have any because we have to buy her medicine. You know, nitroglycerin, and all that."

"Oh, you poor thing." Doctor Schwab faced Lindsey. "How is it remotely possible for you to have ridden the SkyWheel already, Miss O'Day? Why are you not staying with the group? I will be seeking expulsion proceedings against you on Monday morning."

Heat rose into Lindsey's face. Jenna and Meredith pushed her forward.

"Do it, "Jenna said in a whisper.

Lindsey cleared her throat. "Doctor Schwab." Lindsey faltered and cleared her throat again. She swallowed hard. Her whole body shook from cold and fear. Maybe she was sick but it couldn't be the apples this time. Mom had thrown them out. But she certainly felt terrible. She could tell them she didn't feel well and leave. She'd hand Ginger to Meredith and run back to the hotel alone crying. Doctor Schwab interrupted her thoughts.

"I don't think we need a speech from you right now," she said.

Lindsey clinched her fists. Doctor Schwab was too much. She changed her mind. The fact that Doctor Schwab didn't listen wasn't going to stop her any longer. Here goes.

"I think you *do* have to listen to me," Lindsey said. Oh, bother. She pushed her hair behind her ear.

"How dare you—"

"I do dare!" Lindsey pushed her hair back in front of her ear. "Because I am not a member of this group, nor have I ever been a member of this or any group. I am not a student. I am not a guest soloist. I am Jenna's sister."

"Then, who or where is Lisa O'Day?" Doctor Schwab began to look worried. She scanned her clipboard.

"You really should find that out because Lisa O'Day is definitely not me."

Jenna and Meredith hooted and cheered. Jenna stomped her feet and then fell over and scrambled back up.

Doctor Schwab shifted her attention to Jenna. She frowned at her. "Miss Jenna," she said. "How can you cheer after I got you the present for your mother?"

"Sorry, Wilma. But you've been a real booger to my sister."

"Is your mother even sick?"

Lindsey and Jenna nodded solemnly.

"Well, at least that is something."

Something?

Walter stepped in front of Doctor Schwab. "It seems to me that you've messed this up, Schwab. I may have to use the school bylaws against *you*." Doctor Schwab stepped back. Walter then moved forward and inspected Meredith's bundle. "Schwab, obviously this dog is in distress."

"A dog!" Doctor Schwab cried. "That couldn't be the dog from the Food Lion?"

"Yes, it could," Lindsey answered. "It's having babies." A few of the kids in the choir laughed. "Puppies." Let them laugh. She doubted if any of them had stood up to Doctor Schwab.

"Well, tell me what your plan is, young lady?" Walter asked.

"Well, um," Lindsey said.

"Tell him, Lindsey," Jenna poked her. "You know what to do."

"I think … I think we need to get Ginger to a quiet place, back to our hotel room where Meredith can help her. She seems to know a lot about dogs." Lindsey couldn't believe that her voice commanded Walter and Doctor Schwab.

Meredith nodded.

"Excellent decision," Walter said. "Doctor Schwab, please step out of the way of these ladies."

"Oh," Lindsey added. "Could you call my mom's cell phone and tell her, Ellen Rydell, that everything's fine and they should go back to the hotel?"

"I think Doctor Schwab can handle that."

Doctor Schwab nodded, taking down the number on her ever-ready clipboard.

Lindsey started forward but something fell on her back. Chris had draped his high-school letter jacket around her.

"You look pretty cold. Since you've got my hat, you might as well have my jacket." He shrugged.

Lindsey felt faint. She wore a boy's jacket—a jacket, not a hoodie! She pulled her arms through the sleeves of jacket, quilted on the inside and dark wool on the outside with the words Chinowapi High and the number 12 stitched in the brilliant yellow she noticed in the museum. The sleeves flapped down to her thighs and the wool collar scratched her chin. It smelled of deodorant—like ice, wind, and waterfalls. Heaven. Absolute heaven. Tamera never wore a boy's jacket!

"Thanks." Lindsey shook the sleeves. Jenna rolled them up. "I'll give it back to you. And your hat." Jenna shook her head in agreement.

"Whatever." Chris pushed his hands through his hair. He even blushed.

"Let's go," she yelled to Jenna and Meredith, and the three of them ran to the hotel: one wearing high heels that wobbled; another wearing flip flops that didn't flop and a boy's oversized jacket; and a third wearing boots and carrying a pregnant dog. But they were making great strides.

THE MIRACLE OF LIFE

The three girls leaned against the door of room 324, panting after having raced 10 blocks. Lindsey swallowed gulps of stale, unwashed air and rummaged in her pockets for the key card.

"I don't have it. It's in my coat."

Ginger whined from deep within Lindsey's coat.

"I can't take the coat away," Meredith answered. "She's all tangled in it."

"Maybe Mom and Gwen are back." Jenna flipped over and pounded on the door. "Let us in. Let us in. Our dog is dying."

"Jenna!" Meredith and Lindsey both yelled. You could rescue Jenna from danger, but you couldn't change her.

Gwen opened the door. "What took you so long?"

Lindsey rushed past her into the room and stood in front of Mom who lay propped up on the bed.

"Mom, Meredith's dog is having puppies. It's an emergency."

"Go on." Mom sat up and shook out her hair. "I think I deserve more of an explanation."

"I guess I didn't tell you. Sorry."

"Correct, young lady." Mom breathed in deeply. Lindsey knew it well—the sound of Mom's exasperation. She'd been waiting for it all weekend.

"Well, ah, …"

Ginger whined and squirmed in Meredith's arm.

"I'll expect a further explanation from you later," Mom said. "But right now, take care of the dog. Meredith, you know about dogs giving birth?"

Meredith nodded.

"She likes it best in my suitcase." Lindsey pointed to her suitcase on the floor. "She especially likes my pink sweater."

"*Your* pink sweater?" Gwen placed her hands on her hips and examined the suitcase.

"Sorry. *Your* pink sweater. May I borrow it, please?" Lindsey asked.

"Gee, stupid, all you had to do was ask. Go ahead, ruin it."

Jenna smiled her smiley faced smile, "Lindsey named it OPPSOOES."

"You *named* my sweater?" Gwen squinted at Lindsey.

Jenna continued, "And the name means, One Pretty Pink Sweater Owned By—"

"Jenna!" Lindsey shoved Jenna.

"One Excellent Sister." Jenna smiled her smile again. "See, isn't that nice?"

"I have a feeling that wasn't it." Gwen raised her eyebrows.

"I need more towels." Lindsey scurried away, returning with the towels. She tossed her clothes into a pile, except for OPPSOOES —now renamed to pretty pink sweater—which she laid on top of the towels.

Meredith positioned Ginger in Lindsey's pocket of comfort. Ginger's tongue hung out and she panted.

"Water," Lindsey said. "We need water."

"I'll get it." Gwen held up the coffee pot. "Would this be good?"

"No, we need something for Ginger to drink from."

"This." Gwen held up a saucer.

"Yes, great idea. Thanks."

Gwen filled it, and Lindsey placed it in the suitcase next to Ginger. Meredith stretched on a pair of plastic gloves from the sequined bag. She inspected Ginger. No puppies coming yet. The contractions in Ginger's body gained strength, above her stomach, her muscles pulsating, but Ginger lay quiet on her side in a trance.

With nothing left to do, Lindsey collapsed on the scratchy beige carpeting. Gwen, Meredith, and Jenna followed, creating a semi-circle around the suitcase. Gwen acted like she didn't care and Jenna as though she'd explode from worry. Everyone playing their usual role except Lindsey. Lindsey still wore Chris' jacket. She couldn't bear to take it off even as a line of sweat dripped down her back. She inhaled the deodorant smell.

"Where'd you get that jacket?" Gwen asked.

"Chris." Lindsey wanted to burst open with happiness. She wore the jacket of the boy who both Meredith and Gwen wanted.

Gwen sniffed.

Mom and Meredith introduced themselves.

"It's nice to meet you," Mom said. "I'll just take a nap while we wait." Mom crawled under the covers and closed her eyes. Even seeing a dog have puppies couldn't keep her awake.

"She's sick," Lindsey said in a whisper. "Cancer."

"So Jenna wasn't lying to Doctor Schwab?" Meredith asked.

"No. She has non-Hodgkin's lymphoma." The words spilled out of her mouth. She'd finally admitted to Mom's sickness.

"Poor you." Meredith squeezed Lindsey's hand tight.

"I have to decide where I'm going to live while she has her treatments." Lindsey twisted her hair.

"Why don't you live with me?" Meredith flipped her hands open. "I don't have any brothers or sisters and my mom is always busy so you'd make it, well, less lonely."

Jenna leaned in toward Meredith.

"Can I come, too?"

"Well, I don't know, you're kind of young—"

Jenna rolled her eyes. "You sound like Lindsey. Can I have a puppy?"

"Yes, I can say yes to that. Yorkies don't have many puppies though, but you can have one."

"I love you already, Meredith." Jenna hugged her.

Ginger whined and let out a cry. Lindsey put her hand to her heart and crawled near. The other girls mimicked her and crawled nearer too.

"Look, here comes one." Meredith held up Ginger's tail. Half of a black, inky blob emerged but didn't come farther.

"Is it stuck?" Jenna asked. "Help her, Meredith! Help her pull it out."

"No, nobody needs to help her. She does it herself." Meredith rested back on her knees. "Dogs know what to do, Jenna." Meredith smiled at Jenna. Lindsey admired Meredith's calm, just like when she sang.

"It looks like a puppy pod." Lindsey said. "Alien."

Ginger tightened her body again. Meredith lifted Ginger's leg. The blob now grew as large as an egg. Lindsey saw that it was just a thin membrane and underneath it were the eyes and ears of a puppy. The puppy had come no further.

"Help it, Meredith!" Jenna begged. "Help it!"

"Don't worry. It'll come." And, all of a sudden, the little black, inky sack squirted out of Ginger and onto the towel. It didn't move.

"Oh, my gosh, it's dead!" Jenna hugged Lindsey. "I told you to help! I've seen a lot of movies!" Tears pooled in her eyes and her mouth quivered. "It stayed in too long and now it can't breathe in the sack!"

"No, watch," Meredith said. "Ginger will lick off the membrane—the slime."

"Lick it?" Jenna hid her eyes in her arms. "Gross. I'm not looking. Birth is ugly."

Gwen pulled Jenna's arms down. "Jenna, watch. You may never get a chance to see this again." Jenna shook her head. They watched as Ginger licked, tugged, and pulled at the membrane until the silky sack broke open and a moist, dark brown puppy with little orangish claws emerged, his eyes shut tight, and his ears and fur slicked back.

"Another one is coming!" Lindsey cried, as another blob appeared. Ginger delivered two more squirming blobs then licked them clean. The puppies squeaked and squeaked.

"They're hungry brown mice!" Jenna said.

The puppies slithered in the towels rooting blindly for their mother. Meredith picked them up. Ginger sat up her eyes wide and worried until Meredith placed them next to her. She rolled on her side, licking them as they ate.

"Maybe the green goop at the Food Lion was practice for Ginger," Lindsey said. Meredith's forehead crinkled into a frown. Must still be a sore subject. Better never bring it up.

"Did I miss anything?" Mom said, stretching and waking up. "Is it night?" No light filtered through the curtains. Darkness had descended on their only full day at Niagara Falls.

"The puppies are all born. Ginger had three," Gwen told her.

"Three! That's wonderful. Let me see." She leaned over the bed, her curled hair stuck up top of her head in her rooster doo.

"Beautiful. The miracle of life." Mom closed her eyes and tears trickled down her face. *I'm going to help this time!* Lindsey ran back with a tissue.

"Thank you, honey. You've certainly made this a memorable vacation." Lindsey felt her heart sparkle. She'd helped. She'd made it wonderful. She quickly hugged Mom and then sat back down to snuggle with Jenna and watch Ginger.

"How come they're so dark brown, Meredith?" Jenna asked. "Are they a different kind of dog? I want a dog like Ginger. It's the same as Elizabeth Taylor's dog."

"And London Holiday's, too." Meredith nodded.

Lindsey nodded as if she was in on the secret of Canadian things, but maybe someday she would.

"But, Jenna, don't worry," Meredith added. "That's their color when they're born. They change to look more like Ginger in a few weeks."

"OK. Can I take mine home when we leave tomorrow?" Jenna held onto Meredith's arm.

"Sorry, Jenna, the puppies can't leave their mother for at least ten weeks."

"Ten weeks! That's like forever." She fell backward, her knees splayed out. Then she sat back up. "Can I name them?"

"Well, at least your own. Which one are you choosing?"

"That one over there, on the farthest side. The one born first—who I thought was going to die but who was fine. Like my mom will be." Jenna smiled over at Mom. "Do you know if it's a girl or a boy?"

"Well, we don't want to get too close, yet." Meredith examined her hands. "We're not very sterile."

"I knew we should have boiled water," Jenna said. "It's what they do in all the movies."

Lindsey nudged Jenna. "So, what are you going to name her? Why don't you name her Kerrie Kerfuffle? It is what Meredith's grandmother said whenever she was in trouble. That's what this weekend has been, a kerfuffle. We haven't even seen the Falls."

"No, name her Mildred." Gwen laughed. "Or if it's a boy, Horace."

Jenna scowled. "Don't be dumb. I'm naming her Meredith Ellen Lindsey Gwen the fourth."

"Not Doctor Schwab?" Lindsey laughed.

"How are you getting the puppies home?" Gwen asked. She looked at Lindsey and Lindsey knew what Gwen was thinking, "See, Lindsey, you aren't perfect. You didn't figure that out and now you have four dogs in a hotel room." And, Gwen was right. She hadn't.

Knock, knock.

"Who's there?" Jenna sang out.

"A surprise!" the voice said and then there was laughter.

Jenna jumped up. "That voice sounds familiar." She ran to the door.

"Oh, I must look a sight." Mom pushed her curly hair down and got off the bed. "Lindsey, can you bring me my lipstick?" Lindsey trotted over to her purse. Mom's lipstick would make her look like Dracula's wife at the museum, but Lindsey got it for her anyway. Maybe she'd spend Aunt Angie's money to buy Mom a nice light pink.

Jenna opened the door to Aunt Cassie, who wore her plaid poncho, but now she'd added a red and white winter wool hat with straps hanging down. "Don't be mad. I had to come! I missed you guys! It's no fun only having Aunt Angie to talk to. I left a message on my voicemail that I was going to an organic sheep farm to pick up new wool. Do you like my hat?"

"Yes, I do!" Jenna hugged her. "You're rockin' in that hat." Mom and Aunt Cassie kissed cheeks. Aunt Cassie walked into the room. "My, this is Marv's condo?"

"Well, we didn't want to complain," Mom said.

"But it's tacky!" Jenna and Lindsey called.

"Shh!" Meredith said.

"What's going on?" Aunt Cassie removed her coat and hat and set them on the couch. She rubbed her hands together. "Why do we have to be quiet? Why is it so dark? Does Marv's condo have no electricity?"

Knock, knock. Another knock on the door.

"Oh, no, she couldn't have followed me," Aunt Cassie cried.

"Shh!" Meredith said again.

"Maybe it's Dad." Jenna ran to answer it.

In walked Aunt Angie carrying a stack of boxes wrapped in shiny pink, green, and yellow paper with matching bows, stacked perfectly like in a story book. "Hello, hello. I brought lots of presents." She wore a black coat with a fur collar. Meredith's crease appeared between her eyes.

"Cassie, I never thought you'd be here!" Aunt Angie dropped the presents on the bed and hugged Mom.

"You hadn't? Are you sure?" Aunt Cassie hugged Aunt Angie for a brief second—definitely applying the five-second rule. "Isn't that why you showed up?"

"No, of course, not. I thought you were going to a wool farm."

"I did! Do you like my hat?" Aunt Angie held up her winter wool monstrosity.

"I'm sure I don't know because I can hardly see it in this dark." Aunt Angie moved toward the wall switch. "Why aren't the lights on?"

"Don't turn them on!" Meredith pounced up. "Sorry! I mean, shh. We're having puppies. We have to keep it dark. I think you should take off your coat. Ginger might be upset by it."

"And, who, pray tell, are you?" Aunt Angie asked but she obliged by removing her coat and gloves and hanging them in the closet. "May I be introduced to this interesting young lady?"

137

It took a few minutes to explain everything to the aunts. And they had to do their share of ooh-ing and aah-ing over the puppies, but after that the aunts reverted to their number one fun when Aunt Angie said:

"I'll take Meredith home." She fluffed her hair. "I don't have to be anywhere until my hairdresser's on Monday."

"No, I'll take her," Aunt Cassie countered. "Monday we have staff meetings in the morning, which I can surely miss."

"Let me do your nails, Aunt Cassie." Jenna offered. "Sit down here on the couch." Jenna pushed Aunt Cassie down on the couch. "I'll do yours, Aunt Angie, after I'm done with Aunt Cassie's." Jenna displayed the nail polishes: black and purple. "The purple I used on Mom's nails and the black I used on her toes. Which do you like?" Aunt Cassie pointed to the black. "Black! Great choice."

"My car has much more room for the puppies," Aunt Angie said. "I brought my SUV."

"Well, I bought all that new wool. The puppies will love the smell." Aunt Cassie flapped her black nails in the air to dry them.

"Your turn, Aunt Angie," Jenna placed the two bottles of nail polish in front of Aunt Angie. "Pick."

Aunt Angie looked perplexed. "These are my choices?"

"I'll choose for you then." Jenna picked up the black. "You can match Aunt Cassie."

"Yes, dear. That's very nice," Aunt Angie answered. "By the way, speaking of choices, have you girls made your decision?" She waved her hand at the girls.

"Aunt Angie, you have to stay still." Jenna grabbed her hand and put it on the coffee table.

"Oh, sorry, dear. Perhaps the aunt with whom you decide to live should drive you home, and the aunt who loses, I mean, who doesn't get to share in the delight of you girls, drives Meredith back."

"Aunt Angie makes me seem like a booby prize," Meredith whispered to Lindsey. Tears welled in her eyes.

There was another knock on the door.

"Now it has to be Dad!" Jenna ran to answer it. "There's no one left. Who is it?" she sang out as she looked through the peephole. "Oh!" Her hand dropped from the door handle. "It's Walter and Wilma."

"Oh, dear!" Mom ran to the bathroom. "I'll be out in five. Let them in, Jenna."

"Come in, Walter and Wilma," Jenna said.

"Dummy, remember you have to *let* them in," Gwen said.

"Yeah, I *know*. It just sounds cool, like I'm living in a movie. Katherine Hepburn opening the door for Cary Grant not Walter."

Jenna opened the door. Walter entered carrying two large pizza boxes and Doctor Schwab entered carrying sodas.

"We didn't think you could get out for food so we brought some," Walter said. "Puppies born yet?"

"Yes. Ginger had three," Mom answered coming out of the bathroom with more makeup on and her hair combed. "Mother and puppies are doing fine. I'm Ellen. I've heard so much about you." Mom, Walter, and Doctor Schwab shook hands.

"Mind if a few kids come in to see?" Walter asked. Lindsey's heart pumped several unnecessary beats. Behind him, the kids from the choir clustered in the hall.

"Um, no. I don't mind," Mom said. "Please, come in." She beckoned them in.

Aunt Angie and Aunt Cassie hustled over to the kitchen and sat perched on the tilted chairs to let the kids into the tiny condo. Lindsey stood at attention next to Gwen and Meredith as first kids filed in and said, "Hey," to Meredith, then ooh'ed and ahh'ed the puppies. As the kids crowded around Lindsey's suitcase, she prayed an extra prayer that they didn't notice her pile of clothes next to it.

"That's a pretty awesome suitcase," one girl said who wore the usual Chinowapi Choir hoodie but had tied pink ribbons to the end of the strings on her hood. "I've never seen one like that. How did you think to use it for the puppies?"

Lindsey shrugged. How did she think to do that? She wasn't telling.

All the kids finally passed by the puppies and backed out of the room, some saying "Thanks, they sure are cute," and waving goodbye. All that is except Chris and Marcus. He hadn't bothered to come for his hat or letter jacket. How wonderful it would have been to see him again, but now she could wear his jacket to school and tell all the girls in gym class about her boyfriend in Canada and have proof. Then, they'd sit with her at lunch and talk boyfriends and laugh about how crazy in love they were.

A voice called out in the hall. "I can't believe you didn't let me know where you were going." And the lady in the raincoat, Lydia, the soloist, appeared in the doorway. "Hello, hello! These boys were headed down to see puppies and I wanted to see them too. Where are they?"

Lindsey waved her in and she stepped over to the suitcase.

"Oh, my goodness, they do look like rats! Boys, come in, you must see."

Chris and Marcus entered. Lindsey wouldn't have been surprised if a light had shone on them.

"The puppies will be beautiful in a few days, and then I get one," Jenna said. "Do you want your nails done? I'm doing it for all the ladies tonight. Wilma, how about you?"

While Jenna talked in vain and gained no more customers, Chris crossed over to the suitcase and peeked at the puppies with Marcus. She felt her heart drop on the floor as he approached her. She wanted to scramble to pick it up, but instead blushed and took off his jacket.

"Here's your jacket." She handed it to him. "Thanks."

"It's nothing." He hung it across his left shoulder. Oh, her heart thumped back up to her throat. How cool was it to swing a jacket over your shoulder? Oh, she was so far ahead of Tamera. If she could only sneak out her camera and record this moment.

"I'm Jenna." Jenna held out her hand. Chris shook it while smiling a crooked grin. Jenna batted her eyelashes. Was she going to have competition from Jenna too? "I'm sorry I ran away with your hat. I was in a kerfuffle. One of those Canadian kerfuffles, I've heard about."

"That's OK." Chris dropped his hand and stared at her.

"Here it is." And Jenna held out a misshapen, stained, once beautiful hat.

Chris' eyes shot out—his eyes held the exclamation points this time. "Oh, ah, I guess you can keep it."

"That's good," Jenna said. "Because it is pretty much grossed out." Jenna dropped it into the suitcase.

Lindsey searched for Gwen. She stood near Marcus. She laughed and blushed and flipped her hair. Lindsey's eyebrows lifted. Now she knew. Gwen liked Marcus!

"Are you having a party without me?" someone called from the hallway. Dad entered and winked directly at Lindsey.

DECIDING

"I never liked Chris, dweebist of dweebs," Gwen said. "He's so whiney: *I want my hat. I want my hat.* Marcus is more my style. Besides you liked Chris. I wouldn't do that to you."

They'd climbed Clifton Hill again, this time headed to the Falls for their family talk to decide where to live. The aunts had left with Meredith and the puppies, and Dad waited for them at the hotel to drive them home—they'd canceled the limousine and chauffeur. Lindsey had hoped for more kerfuffles: dogs to chase, girls to rescue, boys to well, never mind, but all stayed calm, except for the dread in her stomach. This time they really had to decide.

They walked past the amusements, ignoring the calls to come and play. Overhead the sky frowned on them with more of its dreary November clouds. Gusts of wind teased them but couldn't bother them because Dad had made Jenna leave her hippy hat and had bought them all hoodies—I heart Niagara Falls.

As they continued on, the circus feeling faded. The buildings and street became stately. The tall green glass hotel now rose on Lindsey's left, and she noticed a garden with square-shaped bushes and sidewalks crisscrossing through it, a garden for Prince William and his bride to ride through in their carriage.

Then, she heard it—the Falls roared like the lion of the Food Lion come to life.

"We're here!" Jenna called.

"Yes!" Lindsey caught her hand. "Let's see it together!"

They ran across the park to a fence running along the length of the Falls. They faced the straight American Falls. Its jewel green water rushed over the cliff, crashing down onto the ragged boulders that stood under it, withstanding the pounding. The water flowed into a swirling, churning river deep below, almost matching the churning of Lindsey's stomach. Only that single-bar fence separated them from falling over the bank and into the river. Lindsey stretched her hand across it. "The river keeps us from being near the Falls."

To Lindsey's far left, a bridge spanned the river. Its arch hung *under* the bridge, as if it had slipped and fallen. Like everything in Canada, in a kerfuffle.

To her right, a scattering of tourists stood farther down by the Canadian Falls—the Horseshoe Falls, which matched their name exactly—they bent around a semicircle like a horseshoe, with one end near the fence. Both Jenna and Lindsey pointed at the same time and nodded in agreement. They'd go there. But before they could start, Gwen tapped Lindsey on the shoulder.

"Look. No rides today." Below them, the Maid of the Mist boats, which visitors rode to view under the Falls, lay washed up on shore like a ship wreck, docked for the winter. "We need Dad's submersible."

Lindsey nodded, missing Dad at the thought of him not being with her to see the Falls, and maybe not being with her for the next six months.

Gwen looked around, as if hoping that the kids from the choir would reappear, but Meredith had said the bus left at 6:00 a.m. The choir had sung last night at the Falls, with Lydia and Meredith each singing a solo, and where Chris' ears had glowed fire red, his hat forsaken forever.

Lindsey's face caught the sunlight as it burst through one of the thick November clouds. "It's beautiful."

"It is," Gwen answered, raising her face to the sun as well.

Lindsey ran over and hugged Mom who sat on a bench. "Don't you love the Falls, Mom?"

"Yes, aren't they majestic? Sometimes you see something famous, and it doesn't live up to its fame, but these do. They make me feel the world is large and wonderful. They make Aunt Angie's tacky tourist trap thrilling."

"Jenna and I are going to the Canadian ones."

"I'll come along in a minute." As Lindsey left Mom, she appeared to be deep in prayer, her face now upward to that bit of sun shining through.

"Come on, Jenna," Lindsey called, her voice drowned out by the roar. "The Canadian Falls are bigger than the American. Why did they get the big ones?"

"Maybe because we already had enough big stuff," Jenna yelled back. "You know, the Empire State building and King Kong."

They ran to the very end of the fence, where the far end of the Horseshoe Falls met, and no river separated them from the never-ending rush of water churning to the bottom, only the single green bar fence. The cloud of mist rising from the center of the Horseshoe Falls froze into pellets stinging their eyes and faces.

Lindsey felt the white foam and power of it pound into her chest. It mesmerized her—its fierce determination to fall, fall, fall. Being so near, she could see the bubbles in the white foaming water and feel the spray in her eyes. She imagined the courage it took Annie to go over it in only a barrel and a mattress. She reached out her hand, and then, a bit afraid of its power, stepped back.

"Let's put our foot out under the bar and see how near we can get it to the water," Jenna said. "Maybe we can touch it with our toes."

Lindsey shook her head. "This is close enough."

"Super Lindsey became Super Woos again?"

Jenna glided her foot under the fence toward the Falls. Her heel stuck in a hole and she slid beneath the green bar, only inches away from the Falls, its water sending anyone who dared come over, tumbling to the bottom.

Her dark eyes widened. "Help me, Lindsey! I can't get my shoe out." Jenna pulled and pulled on her foot, sliding a bit closer. "Please, God, don't let me be rushed over the edge."

Lindsey grabbed Jenna's arm and pulled her back. Jenna's high heel fell off and tumbled over the Falls. It spun and swirled in the foam to the bottom, finally lost in the rising mist.

"My shoe!"

Gwen and Mom hurried over.

"Oh, Jenna, dear." Mom hugged her. "What am I going to do with you?"

"If you want to go over the Falls," Lindsey said. "You have to go over it in a barrel or my suitcase." She stood up. "Look," she yelled and pointed at the sky. "Behind you. A rainbow." A perfect rainbow arched across the sky, framing all of the Clifton Hill including the SkyWheel. "That does it, Mom," Lindsey shouted. "I've made my decision."

"You have?" Mom shouted back. "That's great! Let's hear it."

Lindsey started to say but Mom and sisters yelled, "What?" because of the deafening roar of the Falls. They moved near a brick building where Lindsey could see snow globes in the window. Not more snow globes! Jenna hopped over on one foot.

"What were you saying, Lindsey?" Mom asked.

"Jenna can't survive without me. I've got to be where she is."

Jenna hugged Lindsey. "I love you, Linds."

"Corny," Gwen said, and Jenna hugged her, too.

"And, I have to be where Gwen is or she won't have anyone to criticize."

"Oh, really?" Gwen replied.

"But I'm actually not making a decision."

"Lindsey! I so wished you would," Mom said. "You don't want me to decide for you, do you? Like the omelets?"

"No, please, no more omelets. No, I'm not making a decision because there's nothing to decide. I have to be where you are too. We all have to stay together."

"Yeah!" yelled Jenna. "Yeah, yeah, yeah!" And she danced around and then stumbled again.

Lindsey grabbed her shoulders to steady her. "See, we've all got to be here to help each other."

"Tacky," Gwen said. "But I like it."

EPILOGUE –
TEN WEEKS OF WAITING ENDS

Lindsey peered through the window of her living room, waiting. January had wrapped the outside in ice and darkness. The street lights shone cold spotlights down onto the snow-covered street. In the houses next door and across the street, the lights glowed warm as families gathered around their TVs and dinners. The waiting had depleted Lindsey of all her excitement and now she only ached with boredom.

Jenna placed her chin on Lindsey's shoulder. "Maybe they're stuck in a snow pile somewhere, frozen."

A car flashed under a street light. It slowed and turned into their driveway, taking up its entire length and almost scratching their station wagon. Lindsey's face lit up. A limousine! Another limousine arrived at her house! She could only feel sorry for Tamera now. The doors opened and revealed what they'd been waiting for …

Jenna came to life. "She's here. She's here." Jenna screeched down the hall and opened the front door wide. Lindsey, Gwen, and Mom crowded around behind her.

Aunt Angie stepped in carrying a picnic basket wrapped in a red ribbon followed by Aunt Cassie carrying a black box with holes in it tall enough to carry Abe Lincoln's hat.

"Ellen, you look lovely." Aunt Angie air kissed Mom on both cheeks as if she were French and as if it had been weeks since she had seen her instead of two days ago.

"You look delightful." Aunt Cassie squeezed Mom in a bear hug. Aunt Angie stepped back and hugged Mom as well.

Jenna shoved past the aunts. "Meredith! Meredith! How are you? Mom doesn't have any hair anymore and she keeps teasing me she's going to wear my dog as a wig. I'm too old for that stuff."

"Oh, Jenna," Mom said. "Welcome, Meredith. Glad you could come." In place of Mom's curly hair, she wore a bright pink cap covered in flowers and feathers that Jenna and Lindsey had made. Her bones showed through her translucent skin, frail and thin. Lindsey stood behind her, with her hand on her arm.

"Thank you, Mrs. Rydell," Meredith entered. She wore another lumberjack outfit but with a pink ribbon in her hair. She nodded at Gwen. "Hi." Then, she took the black box from Aunt Cassie and handed it to Jenna. "Here's Horace Claude Oscar George the sixteenth." Meredith laughed.

"Yeah, yeah, yeah!" Jenna danced with the box.

"Jenna hasn't slept all night, Meredith, waiting for you," Mom said. "Lindsey either." Lindsey groaned. Mom was as bad as Jenna at telling on her. "Jenna, sit on the couch before you open it so the poor dog doesn't drop on the floor."

Lindsey shoved a dark purple plaid blanket off the couch to make room for Meredith. The aunts perched on the arms of the couch, each protesting that they were very comfortable, and Aunt Angie protesting that she was the most comfortable of all. Meredith scanned the orange plastic medicine bottles strewn across the coffee table and the glasses half full of water, a medicine junkyard. Gwen settled on the other side of the room in an armchair.

147

Jenna held up a bottle. "See, this is the medicine you take to stop from throwing up." She held up a second. "Which is what happens when you take this one."

"That's interesting, Jenna." Meredith winced.

"No nitroglycerin." Jenna waved at the medicine. "I might have told you that. I was exaggerating."

"Well, we all do that especially when we're upset." Meredith nudged Jenna. "I may have done that to Lindsey, as well, maybe, a bit at the Food Lion." She tilted her head at Lindsey and Lindsey knew it was an apology. Lindsey smiled at Meredith. An apology that was accepted! Meredith continued, "Oh, this basket is from my mother, Mrs. Rydell. She wanted to come but she was called into court for a special session with the judge. So, I came by myself." Meredith frowned.

"With your new aunts!" Aunt Cassie said. "We consider you our fourth niece!"

Meredith smiled only a bit. Lindsey wondered how happy Meredith was at that prospect.

"Well, thank you and your mother." Mom opened the basket and added the items, one after another to the clutter on the coffee table. "Look everyone. Cheese from England, wheat crackers, and Brazilian coffee. That was so kind of your mother."

Only Jenna's gift remained unopened but she sat still, almost prayerful, with her hands in her lap. Lindsey couldn't believe she wasn't tearing open the box.

"Open the box, Jenna." Lindsey poked Jenna. "Let's see your dog. I'll even get Chris' hat for her. Or my suitcase." The dog's scratching inside the box and pushing against the sides reminded Lindsey of how Ginger had done that inside her coat. It made her ache for Ginger and become more excited for Jenna to open the box to reveal her offspring.

"No, I can't open it yet. I've got to think." Jenna stopped and studied each of them, girls, aunts, and Mom. "Remember how it seemed that we were going to lose everything. Now look. We've even got Meredith. Can you stay forever, Meredith?"

"Well, I don't know."

"You can't sound like Lindsey. You've got to decide," Jenna said.

"You open up your gift, and I'll decide."

Jenna ripped off the top the box. Inside sat a miniature Ginger, so tiny two of her could fit in Chris' hat. Lindsey reached to pet her only to find her hand blocked by Jenna's, Gwen's, and her aunts'. The dog barked a squeaky mouse bark and scrambled with its sharp nails to get out of the box.

"Will this poor thing survive so much love?" Mom asked and then answered her own question. "I did these past few months so a dog certainly can."

Jenna placed Meredith Ellen Lindsey Gwen on the ground to play. The little dog jumped and bit at Jenna's hand. Jenna laughed.

"You know, I could have bought Jenna a dog long ago." Aunt Angie reached for the dog and put it on her lap.

"Well, I could have found one at a rescue shelter." Aunt Cassie took the dog from Aunt Angie. "It's much better to adopt one than to go to a breeder. There are so many lost dogs."

"I didn't say I wouldn't go to a rescue shelter." Aunt Angie took back the dog only to have Jenna take it and place it back on the floor. "I just said that I could have bought her one."

"Well, I brought some organic dog food." Aunt Cassie pulled up a bag of dog food from behind the couch so big that Meredith Ellen Lindsey Gwen would be eating it for years.

"I bought a lovely vintage pearl collar for her." Aunt Angie dug in her purse and held up a collar that was studded with pearls and large enough for a Doberman pincher. Jenna put it on her wrist and admired it in the light.

"So, how's Doctor Schwab?" Lindsey asked Meredith. "Still after you?"

"No. Demoted!" Meredith laughed. "She's now the assistant to the assistant principal. No more chaperoning, only patrolling the halls of the high school."

"She'll like that. Doctor Schwab is always on patrol." Lindsey laughed.

"Is there anyone else you want to ask about at Chinowapi High?" Meredith asked.

"Oh, I don't think so." Lindsey blushed and twisted her hair.

"Well, I'll tell you anyway." Meredith nudged her. "Chris helped the Chinowapi High basketball win finals."

Now that she knew about Chris, she realized she didn't care. Chris had become a faded fairytale, the most unreal part of their girls' weekend. What had been real and fun had been their adventures of going over the Falls in a suitcase—together.

"And, Marcus moved to Quebec," Meredith added.

"Quebec!" Gwen cried. She pulled on her blonde streak.

"He'll be French!" Lindsey rolled off the couch, laughing. "French. Gwen will have to marry him now. Quebec is as close to France as she'll ever get."

"Tacky, Linds," Gwen said, with stars in her eyes like Dr. Schwab.

"How are you feeling, Mrs. Rydell?" Meredith asked, looking at Mom's cap.

"Call me Ellen. I've finished my treatment. My hair is even growing back. Look." She took off the cap to show her hair, a super short hairdo perfect for the Army. "Feel. It's prickly."

"Mom!" Gwen said.

"It's life, Gwen. You've got to live it. I'm done crying."

Dad came in from the garage. "So Meredith, we meet again. Welcome." He held his hand to Meredith and she pumped it. "I hope you can stay for a while and be like one of the family. There's too much pink in this house. We need a little tomboy."

"Well, I could buy everyone a lumberjack shirt," said Aunt Angie.

"I could make them out of organic cotton," said Aunt Cassie.

"Make one for me too," Dad said. "I'll take mine in purple." He winked. Lindsey heart swelled. Dad hadn't winked very much in the last few weeks.

"Dad," Gwen said. "You are being sexist and perpetuating stereotypes. Very culturally insensitive."

"That's what I'm always trying to do," he replied, winking at Gwen.

"You know," Aunt Angie said. "That is a project we could work on together."

"Really?" Aunt Cassie fell off the couch. "We could work together?"

"Sure, I could buy the material and you could sew them."

"Why, Angie—" Aunt Cassie grabbed a tissue and cried.

"You guys are more fun when you're fighting," Gwen said.

"So what should we have for dinner?" Dad asked, squeezing in between Mom and Jenna and patting Meredith Ellen Lindsey Gwen the fourth. "I can cook, if you'd like Meredith."

Meredith's eyes darted around. "Oh, um ..."

Meredith needed help, and Lindsey would help her, this and every time. "No, Meredith." Lindsey shook her head. "You don't want him to cook. One time when Mom was sick, he made Coke-flavored rice, another time he put pork chops in spaghetti. He called it mystery meat and we had to guess what kind it was."

"Well, I don't know what's wrong with that," Dad said. "I was thinking of horseradish sauerkraut for tonight. How does that sound?" He winked again at Meredith. Dad was making up for his winking today!

Meredith squinted and grimaced. "I guess, pretty good, Mr. Rydell."

"I could whip us up tofu sloppy joes," Aunt Cassie echoed.

"I could call François and ask him to come over and make his signature dish," Aunt Angie said. "It's—"

"Stop!" Lindsey cried. "I'll call for a pizza! And, I'll decide what's on it!" She winked at Dad who winked back. Meredith Ellen Lindsey Gwen the fourth barked.

ABOUT THE AUTHOR

Kathy Vincenz is the author of *Over the Falls in a Suitcase* and many articles and short stories. She lives on a hill with her husband, children, and many squirrel friends, who are fed everything from bread to taco chips. She is also a technical writer and explains how to use software to help solve engineering problems.